RANGER JUSTICE

TEXAS RANGER HEROES

LYNN SHANNON

RANGER JUSTICE

Whoever does not love does not know God, because God is love.

1 John 4:8

ONE

A faint thump came from downstairs.

Hannah Lawson sat straight up in bed. Her heart raced as she strained to listen for more sounds. Had someone broken in? Or was her imagination playing tricks on her? She'd been in that drifting-off state, the place right before falling to sleep, and it was possible her mind had manufactured the noise. Wind rattled the windows panes and thunder boomed in the distance. A storm was rolling in. Perhaps that had woken her.

Silence followed. No intruder had invaded her home. Hannah let go of the breath she was holding and silently admonished herself for overreacting. The death threats she'd received recently were stressing her out. As an assistant district attorney for Fulton County, it was her job to represent the state against criminals who harmed citizens. She took pride in her job. Loved it. But these last few months had been difficult.

A quick glance at the clock confirmed she'd only been

in bed for half an hour. The baby monitor glowed, Charlotte's tiny form still in her crib. The six-month-old was an excellent sleeper. Thank goodness. Hannah rose from the bed and, on bare feet, drifted into the nursery. The scent of baby powder hung heavy in the air. It soothed her nerves and tugged a smile from her lips.

Her niece lay center in the crib, dressed in a sleep sack with sheep dancing across the fabric. Charlotte's arms were thrown above her head. A silky curl played with one chubby cheek. Tender affection swept through Hannah. She'd never imagined juggling single-motherhood, but lately, that's what she was doing. Her brother and sister-in-law were both Marines. The military tried to avoid deploying married couples at the same time, especially when they had children, but there were times it was unavoidable. Her brother, Ben, was a year into his orders with another two months to go. Her sister-in-law left three weeks ago on hers.

Hannah had been the only family member capable of taking care of Charlotte in the interim. Although juggling the baby's care with her demanding job was difficult, it was also a blessing. This was probably the closest she'd ever come to having a child of her own. She'd lost her husband five years ago in a war zone an ocean away. Patrick had been best friends with her brother. They'd gone through boot camp together and were stationed at the same base. When Hannah met him, she was in her third and final year of law school. Their romance was a slow burn, but Patrick had won her over with his steadiness and humor.

Falling in love with him had been simple. Losing him had nearly broken her.

She swiped at an absent tear that trickled down her cheek. Grief had a way of creeping up unexpectedly. Or maybe her brother's recent deployment was triggering all of those old emotions. Ben, his wife Danielle, and Charlotte were the only family she had left in the world. Her dad died when she was in elementary school, her mom shortly after college. She couldn't imagine losing her only sibling too.

She sent up a silent prayer for Ben's continued safety, along with her sister-in-law's. Then Hannah pressed a kiss to her fingers before brushing them against Charlotte's head. "Sweet dreams, sweetie."

Hannah backed away from the crib and quietly slipped from the room. Her mind swirled with thoughts. Sleep was an impossibility now. Insomnia had plagued her for most of her adult life, and recently, it'd gotten worse. Stress did that.

More thunder rumbled, and a streak of lightning illuminated the staircase. She had a full day of work tomorrow. Maybe some warm milk would help. She hurried to the lower level and into the kitchen. Papers littered the table next to her laptop. Hannah studied the crime scene photos again.

Julie Anderson. She'd been stabbed to death in her own home. Her husband, a local doctor, had been arrested for the crime. His trial began next week, and was already receiving widespread media attention. As the prosecutor, Hannah was in charge of presenting the case to the jury. The weight of responsibility bearing down on her shoulders was heavy. She wanted to bring Julie's killer to justice. Unfortunately, the case was complicated and emotions among the community were running high. Hannah had received numerous death threats in the last few weeks.

Rain pattered against the roof as the storm picked up. Hannah retrieved the milk from her fridge, but a sound from the living room sent her heart rate spiking again. She froze. The hair on the back of her neck rose as she sensed someone in her home. It was an indescribable feeling. One not based on logic, but on a primitive intuition.

Another scrape came from around the corner. The sound of a boot against the wood floor. Hannah's panic took flight. Her gaze shot to the mudroom, narrowing in on the security panel next to the door.

It was dark. Unarmed.

Impossible. She'd set it before going to bed. Someone —the intruder—had overridden it.

Lightning shot across the sky, followed by an impressive boom of thunder. Hannah swallowed back a scream. She eased the milk onto the counter before slipping a knife out of the wooden block. The handle of the blade was cold against the heat of her skin.

Keeping her ears pricked for any sound coming from the dark living room, Hannah reached for her cell, charging next to the coffee machine. She quickly dialed 911. The operator picked up on the first ring. Hannah kept her voice pitched low as she identified herself and provided her address. "There's an intruder in my home. Send the police."

She eased toward the staircase, never turning her back on the living room. Her hand clutched the knife. Tremors threatened to weaken her knees as another footstep creaked the wooden floor. The area beyond the kitchen was pitch-black, shapes indistinguishable, her view partially blocked by the doorframe.

She needed to get upstairs. The knife was better than nothing, but Hannah was no fool. Whoever had entered her home had evil intentions. Charlotte was alone, innocent and vulnerable. She had to protect her niece. The best option was to lock themselves in a bathroom upstairs until help arrived.

Hannah eased onto the first step. Then the second. Her heart ricocheted against her rib cage. *Please, God, help me.*

A man appeared in the kitchen doorway. Dressed all in black and wearing a ski mask. Terror streaked through Hannah. She lifted the knife and said, "Don't come any closer. The police are on their way."

He froze. She prayed the intruder would retreat, and for one heart-stopping moment, it seemed he considered it. Then, with a growl, he lunged for her.

Hannah screamed, dropping the phone. It clattered to the carpet while she lashed out with the knife as the intruder tackled her. Pain vibrated through her body as her back collided with the steps. Her head rapped against the railing. Stars danced across her vision.

The attacker gripped her throat with meaty fingers,

constricting her airway, as he slammed her other hand against the staircase. The knife fell from her grip. Hannah formed a fist with her other hand, and using muscles toned from years of Pilates, punched him in the face.

The impact sang up her arm as agony erupted along her knuckles. He fell back long enough for her to suck in a breath. Hannah scrambled to get out from underneath him. She kicked and lashed out with all the panic and fury of a trapped animal. Some of her hits landed. Others didn't. But it was enough to scoot herself away from him. Hannah stumbled to her feet. She turned to race up the stairs.

A vise gripped her ankle. Hannah hit the staircase with a violent jolt that rattled her teeth. Her body slid down the few stairs she'd managed to climb. She grappled for the upper hand, but her petite frame was no match for his brute strength. The attacker fisted her hair and twisted her head back until she feared it would snap off her body.

Then the icy touch of a blade kissed her neck.

TWO

Wind whipped raindrops as Texas Ranger Ryker Montgomery maneuvered his way through dozens of police vehicles to the crime scene. The house was two stories with clean lines and a well-kept yard. A plastic baby swing hung from the arm of a giant oak tree. The sight of it made his chest tighten. Dispatch hadn't shared much with Ryker about the crime scene, only that it was high profile and he was needed immediately.

He sent up a silent prayer heavenward. Children were a tender spot for any law enforcement officer, but Ryker had a special built-in rage for criminals that hurt or endangered kids. The bullet wound along his left side burned with a phantom pain. It'd been nearly thirty years since Ryker's girlfriend, Alison, was murdered during a gas station robbery. He'd nearly lost his life as well when the killer shot him. They'd been fifteen. Riding their bicycles home from the lake after spending the afternoon swimming.

Alison had wanted a soda and a chocolate bar. She'd paid with her life.

"Ryker." Gavin Sterling raised a hand in greeting from his place on the front porch. His colleague wore the official Texas Ranger uniform: khakis, white button-down, and cowboy boots. His dark hair was covered by a hat and a wedding band encircled the ring finger on his left hand.

Surprise flickered through Ryker as he shook his friend's hand. "Are you back from your honeymoon already? I thought you had another week."

"So did I, but Jacob started running a high fever a few days ago and Claire was worried, so we cut our trip short." Gavin was married to the Fulton County sheriff. Her son from a previous marriage, Jacob, was everything to the couple. "Thankfully, it was just a bad bout of the flu. His fever broke last night."

"I'm glad he's okay." Ryker provided his name to the officer at the front door for the crime scene log and then removed a set of booties from a box. He slipped them over his damp cowboy boots. "Is Claire here?"

"She's inside." Gavin handed Ryker a set of latex gloves. "Bennett is helping Luke with a double homicide, so I volunteered to take the lead on this."

Ranger Bennett Knox and Ranger Luke Tatum were part of their team. Bennett normally handled cases in Fulton County, but there were times the rangers in Company A assisted each other with investigations. Ryker and Gavin had both filled in for him when he was called away. Like now. It was one benefit of having a close-knit group.

Ryker tugged on a set of latex gloves. "What do we have?"

"Break-in and attempted murder. Looks like a target hit." Gavin frowned. "This house belongs to assistant district attorney, Hannah Lawson."

That name drew Ryker up short. His gaze shot to the interior of the house, but there was no sign of the redheaded beauty. Dread swirled in his belly. "Was she hurt? What about Charlotte?"

"The baby is fine. Hannah's got some bumps and bruises. She and the intruder fought. He got the upper hand and held a knife to her throat, but deputies arrived on the scene and knocked on the door. It was enough to distract the would-be killer. Hannah got free without having her throat slashed, but her attacker escaped."

Anger pulsed through Ryker's veins. He didn't cotton to any woman being assaulted, but Hannah being attacked sparked his temper in a new way. They'd worked on several cases together since she'd joined the Fulton County District Attorney's Office. Ryker had grown to admire her deep commitment to her job and her family. "Take me through the scene."

Gavin escorted Ryker inside. The home was decorated in pastel walls. A comfy sofa and bookcases created an inviting living room. Sheriff Claire Wilson—no, now she was Claire Sterling—stood in the corner of the room, observing a crime scene investigator as he coated a window ledge with black dust. Glass was scattered on the beige carpet. Claire offered Ryker a tight smile. "Not the best welcome home after my honeymoon."

"No." He gestured to the broken window. "Is that how the intruder got in?"

"Yep. The home has a security system, which he bypassed. Probably with some kind of jammer. Then he broke the window and entered the house." Claire strolled to the staircase. Her blond hair was tied back into a tight ponytail and her shoulders were damp from being out in the rain. "This leads up to the second floor. There are two staircases in the house. My guess is, he went upstairs looking for Hannah after breaking in using the one off the living room, but she took the rear staircase into the kitchen around the same time. They missed each other."

Ryker pictured it in his mind. "Okay, then what happened?"

"He realized Hannah was downstairs and used the same staircase to come into the living room. Hannah was in the kitchen." Claire tilted her head to indicate Ryker should follow her. They went past a dining room and through a doorway into a spacious kitchen with a large center island. Crime scene investigators were photographing the room. Drops of blood, identified with bright yellow markers, spotted the tile floor. "The attacker jumped her while Hannah was attempting to escape up the staircase."

"How did she know someone was in the house?"

"She heard the intruder when he came back down the stairs. She called 911 and grabbed a knife." Claire's expression darkened. "The intruder disarmed her and then used that same knife to threaten her." She held up her thumb and forefinger within a breath of each other. "Hannah was this close to having her throat cut."

Ryker felt that same heat rise in his veins. He wasn't known for having a temper—the exact opposite, in fact. Nothing riled him, but this time, couldn't quite contain his response. "Fingerprints?"

"None yet. Hannah said the guy was wearing gloves, so I'm not hopeful. Officers searched the outside of the home, especially near the broken window, but the storm erased any potential foot impressions." She waved toward the blood spots. "We might get lucky with DNA. Hannah nailed some solid hits when she fought back. If the attacker is in the federal or local databases, we'll identify him."

"I'll submit the paperwork." Ryker glanced at Gavin. "Can you take it directly to the lab? Put a rush on it."

"Absolutely."

Ryker nodded his thanks. One benefit of being a Texas Ranger was that their cases got priority. DNA normally took weeks. In this case, it could be days. Catching Hannah's attacker was essential. She was a prosecutor and a threat on her life was taken as seriously as one made on a fellow police officer.

"You should interview Hannah ASAP." Claire held Ryker's gaze. "She's got information you'll want to hear. She's upstairs."

His brow arched. "Okay." He glanced at Gavin and then back at Claire. "Anyone want to give me a heads-up on what I'm walking into?"

11

"Hannah specifically asked to explain it to you."

Nerves jittering, Ryker took the stairs two at a time to the second floor. Officer Jenkins—Claire's newest hire—guarded a closed door. She shot Ryker a flirtatious smile, one he might've returned at any other time, but not now. His mind was solely focused on finding out whatever mysterious secret Hannah was holding onto. He knocked and paused momentarily before opening the door.

It was a nursery. Decorated in pale pink and lavender, with a large picture window and a crib. The name Charlotte was hung with wooden letters on one wall. Toys spilled from a corner basket. The overhead light was off, but there was enough of a glow from a corner lamp to bathe the room in soft illumination.

Hannah turned as Ryker entered. Her curvy form was encased in a pencil skirt and a silk blouse. Probably not what she'd worn to bed. She must've dressed before his arrival after her injuries were photographed and her pajamas taken into evidence. Hair the color of a shiny new penny framed a porcelain face stunning enough to stop any man in his tracks. A high forehead was offset by a perfectly shaped mouth. Dainty freckles skipped across her nose. She was petite, barely coming up to his shoulder, but heels added another few inches.

They were work colleagues and acquaintances. Ryker knew some things about her personal life. She was widowed. Visited Fulton County on vacation, fell in love with the town, and moved here looking for a fresh start after a hectic career as a prosecutor in Austin. Attended the same church as Ryker and his parents. Her older brother was in the military and currently deployed. So was his wife. Hannah had taken temporary custody of their daughter, Charlotte, for a few months.

She was also an outstanding lawyer. Since joining the DA's office, Hannah had successfully prosecuted or plea-bargained hundreds of cases. Ryker had been impressed by her dedication and her integrity. She never cut corners, nor was she afraid of risks. She fought for justice every time.

Despite his attraction and his admiration, Ryker resisted deepening their relationship to something more. When her gaze met his, he was reminded why. The pierce of those icy blue orbs cut straight through him. Hannah was the only woman he'd ever met who made him feel… unbalanced. As if she saw every insecurity and wound buried in his psyche. He didn't like it.

"Thanks for coming so quickly, Ryker." Hannah kept her voice pitched low to prevent from waking the baby. She absently touched the cross pendant hanging from a delicate gold necklace with trembling fingers. Several knuckles on her right hand were scraped raw and swollen.

The sight punctured through the wall he normally kept up around Hannah. She was trying to hold it together, but was struggling. Rightfully so. He crossed the room and, without thinking, cupped her shoulder with his palm. "Are you okay? Do you need to see EMS?"

She shook her head. "No."

"Can I call someone for you?"

"Gavin already took care of it. Pam is on her way over."

Pam Westgrove was a paralegal in the District Attorney's office. The older woman was something akin to a surrogate grandmother. She'd known Hannah's mother back in Austin, if memory served, and their families had been close for decades. Pam was the only family Hannah had nearby now that her brother and sister-in-law were deployed.

A wail came from the corner of the room. Charlotte made her presence known loud and clear. Tiny fists waved in frustration. Hannah raced to the baby's side and cooed before lifting her out of the crib. She cuddled the little one close to her chest. Something inside Ryker twisted hard watching the steel-boned lawyer morph into a warm caregiver. He'd seen this side of Hannah before, with the families of murdered victims, but witnessing her with a baby punched differently somehow.

Charlotte quieted. The infant was sweet with tendrils of dark hair and a button nose.

Hannah continued rocking her side to side even as her attention locked back on Ryker. "How confident are you that Doctor Anderson killed his wife?"

Ryker was knocked momentarily speechless by her question. Julie Anderson was found stabbed to death in her home by her husband, Thomas. He claimed to have gone to the grocery store and returned to find her murdered. In actuality, he'd killed his wife. His trial started next week. Hannah was the lead prosecutor. Ryker blinked, confusion mingling with a heavy sense of trepidation. "I'm certain he killed her. Why are you asking?"

She held his gaze. "Because the man who attacked me..." Uncharacteristic tears shimmered in her eyes and Hannah sucked in a breath to hold them back. A moment later, she cleared her throat. "He claims to be Julie Anderson's killer."

Ryker's mouth dropped open. "How do you know that?"

She pointed to a piece of paper encased in an evidence bag. "He left a note."

THREE

Hannah cuddled her niece closer as she deftly made a bottle using the supplies kept in the nursery for emergency feedings. Charlotte was going through a growth spurt and occasionally woke for a late-night snack. The routine provided comfort. Normalcy. Hannah could almost pretend tonight's events hadn't happened.

Almost... but not quite. It was only midnight, but it felt like Hannah had been up for days. Her head ached from being slammed against the stairs and her muscles were sore from the beating she'd taken by the attacker. And that was only the physical aspects. It would take weeks, if not months, to recover from the emotional impact of having her home invaded. Her niece put at risk. She shuddered thinking about how close evil had been to the precious baby in her arms.

Hannah settled into the rocking chair and tilted the bottle for Charlotte. Once she was assured the baby was eating properly, her gaze drifted to Ryker. He was still studying the letter. His towering height—over six foot two—and broad shoulders commanded attention. A permanent five-o'clock shadow covered his chiseled jaw. Greek ancestry provided him with an olive skin tone and cheekbones that appeared carved from granite. The man was stunningly gorgeous. And he knew it. Ryker was a notorious flirt. Hannah wasn't much for office gossip, but even a blind and deaf woman would've been hard pressed to avoid learning about his reputation.

She didn't give a fig what Ryker did in his personal life, but work... that was a different matter altogether. Hannah had kept him at arm's length initially but, over time, was pleased to discover he was an excellent Texas Ranger. One of the best. Yes, there was a rakish edge to his personality, but it was tempered with a fierce dedication to victims and their families.

A slow-growing friendship developed from there. Hannah wouldn't consider them close, but they'd spent hours working on cases together. Law enforcement's role was to examine the evidence and interview persons of interest, but prosecutors determined if there was enough probable cause to charge a suspect. Sometimes, the relationship required working together to gather enough evidence.

She'd gleaned some personal information from their interactions. Ryker was close to his family, took his Christian faith seriously, and collected friends like a kid gathered shells from the beach. He was quick to laugh and slow to anger. A straight-shooter, in every sense of the word, and trustworthy.

Hannah had a hard time believing the contents of the letter in Ryker's hand were true. But she couldn't ignore the possibility. The intruder had dropped it while escaping. She imagined he'd intended to leave it near her body, but their altercation hadn't gone as planned. Thank God.

Her attention focused back on the man standing in the center of the room. "Is there any truth to that letter?" Hannah was careful to keep judgment or recrimination out of her tone. "Any chance Dr. Anderson is innocent of killing his wife?"

Ryker met her gaze. His eyes were a tangle of green, blue, and brown. As complicated as the man. His jaw hardened. "Not in my opinion." He blew out a breath. "You've seen the evidence. His wife was pregnant. He didn't want the baby because he was in the midst of having an affair. There was also no prenup. A divorce would've been costly, child support too."

"Yes, but Dr. Anderson claims he was at the grocery store during the time his wife was killed."

"No one at the market remembered seeing him. He didn't have a receipt, nor could the store produce one for the items found in the grocery sacks found in the Anderson kitchen on the night of the murder." Ryker's nostrils flared. "The items Thomas supposedly purchased were nonperishable. He could've bought them days before in order to create a credible alibi."

She agreed with him. In theory. The evidence had been strong enough to warrant bringing charges, but there were holes. "Dr. Anderson has maintained his innocence. According to his deposition testimony, a drug dealer threatened him in the parking lot of his office one week prior to Julie's murder. The guy identified himself only as Cash." The police had done a composite sketch of the suspect, but no one matching the description had ever been found. "Cash wanted Dr. Anderson to write narcotics prescriptions for fake patients, and when he refused, the man became irate and threatened him before finally leaving. Dr. Anderson believes Julie was killed in retaliation."

Ryker snorted. "Right. The mysterious drug dealer. If the good doctor was so terrified by this encounter, why didn't he call the police? He never reported it. I think the entire incident was made up." He glanced down at the letter in his hand. "This is addressed to me specifically."

"You were the lead investigator in Julie Anderson's murder."

He nodded, his attention never leaving the type-written letter as he read it aloud. "Ranger Montgomery, it's been amusing to watch you stumble around trying to uncover the truth about Julie's murder. I considered letting her husband take the fall for me, but I'm tired of staying in the shadows. I want the world to see me. Catch me if you can." He glanced at Hannah holding the baby, and his jaw tightened again. "The intruder intended to kill you in the same manner as Julie, and then leave this note behind. How convenient for Thomas Anderson."

Hannah wasn't surprised by his sarcastic tone, but there was an edge to his words she hadn't heard before. An anger. A protectiveness. For her? Surely not. Ryker had never indicated he found her attractive or was interested in her romantically. Nor did she want him to. That would open a can of worms she wasn't prepared to mess with.

She set the empty bottle down on the small table next to the rocking chair and shifted Charlotte onto her shoulder to burp her. The baby was fast asleep, her long eyelashes resting on chubby cheeks. Hannah patted her back while continuing to rock gently, but placed her focus on Ryker's assertion. "You're suggesting that Thomas hired someone to murder me in the same manner as his wife in order to prove his innocence?" Another involuntary shudder rippled through Hannah as her mind flashed back to the feel of the knife blade against her throat. Julie Anderson had been stabbed several times before her throat was cut. She'd bled out in a manner of minutes. "That's a stretch, isn't it?"

"Not for Thomas. The man is a sociopath and a narcissist. He'll do whatever it takes to stay out of prison and is convinced he's smarter than us." Ryker frowned. "You have to tell the defense attorney about this letter, don't you?"

"Of course." The rules of discovery required Hannah to turn over any evidence that could prove exculpatory to the defendant's counsel. She sighed. "The defense's entire strategy is based on the drug dealer retaliation theory."

He waved the note. "Which this falls into perfectly."

His theory was valid. Still, Hannah had a job to do, and she wouldn't assume anything. "We have to treat this note as valid and run a full investigation. Quick. The

Anderson trial is scheduled to begin next week. If I were the opposing counsel, I'd bring this note to the judge's attention in a pretrial motion and ask for the charges against my client to be dropped."

Ryker's gaze hardened. "Do you plan on dropping the charges?"

"Of course not. There was sufficient probable cause to charge Thomas with the murder of his wife, and like you, I believe he's guilty. But what I believe and what I can prove in a court of law are two different things. And we can't be seen taking sides or attempting to ignore evidence that's right in front of us."

Charlotte took that moment to let out a belch and Hannah couldn't help but smile. "That wasn't very ladylike."

Ryker chuckled. The low baritone vibrated his chest and twisted Hannah's insides in a strange way. "She's cute." The mirth fled from his expression as quickly as it came. "If we're right, and Thomas is behind this attack on you, then he may not be done."

Icy fear washed over Hannah. She swallowed hard. "What are you talking about? If he is behind this, then the note accomplishes what he wants. To create reasonable doubt."

Criminal trials required the prosecutor to prove "beyond a reasonable doubt" that the defendant was guilty. If the jury had any logical misgivings, then they needed to acquit. It was a high bar. Hannah wasn't sure—even before the letter—that she could pull off a conviction in this case. After his wife's murder, Thomas had conducted a thorough and effective media campaign. His willingness to do interviews, and his charming personality, had convinced a large swath of the population of his innocence.

But like Ryker, Hannah had seen through the veneer of Thomas's exterior. He was a master manipulator. His alibi was too carefully concocted, the grief over losing his wife too calculated. Their marriage had been on the rocks for a while. Thomas had been having, according to witnesses, a heated love affair with his nurse. Julie had considered divorce, but then found out she was pregnant.

One month later, she was murdered.

Ryker leveled a look at Hannah. "As the lead prosecutor in this case, you determine whether to pursue a murder charge or not. You've been a thorn in Thomas's side from day one. If you're..."

"Dead." She met his gaze head-on, her chin tilted up. Talking about this terrified her, but she wouldn't run from the danger, nor would she be scared away from doing her job. "Don't sugarcoat, Ryker. I can take it."

He hesitated and then nodded. "If you're killed, then another prosecutor will be assigned to the case. Someone who may be more amenable to dropping the charges." A muscle in his jaw twitched. "I don't think it was an accident you were attacked. Thomas wants you gone. At a minimum, he wants you frightened."

"I don't scare easily." She rose from the rocking chair and crossed to the crib before laying Charlotte down on the mattress. The baby sighed with contentment. Light played along the delicate features of her sweet face, the rosebud mouth and soft chin.

Love swelled inside her. It was a reminder of why Hannah was so committed to her work. She wanted the world to be a safer place for her niece. That required bravery. Facing down bad people and bringing them to justice so they couldn't hurt others wasn't easy, but it was her calling.

She turned to face Ryker. "I have no intention of backing down."

His gaze flickered to the baby behind her before returning to Hannah's. Determination rode his strong features. "Then the two of you will need my protection."

FOUR

Morning dew coated the grass as Ryker finished a perimeter check around Hannah's property. He'd spent most of the night keeping watch after the crime scene investigators left. His boss, Lieutenant Vikki Rodriquez, had officially assigned him to protect Hannah while other rangers in Company A, in coordination with the Fulton County Police Department, worked on neutralizing the threat against her. Claire had stationed police officers at the beginning of the neighborhood to keep the media away. Despite their best efforts, someone had leaked the attack and the contents of the letter to a reporter.

The scent of fresh coffee and eggs greeted Ryker as he stepped into the mudroom. He slipped off his boots and went into the kitchen. Pam, an apron wrapped around her ample waist, stood at the stove. She'd spent the night in the guest bedroom. Her gray hair was neatly pulled back into clips, her face scrubbed free of makeup.

She greeted Ryker with a smile. "Morning. Hope you like breakfast burritos."

"I like everything." He beelined for the coffee machine and poured a cup of the dark brew. The smell alone began clearing the fog from his brain. "Are Hannah and Charlotte still sleeping?"

"No, they're up and getting ready for the day." Pam glanced at her watch and then turned off the stove. "I'd better get a move on. I've gotta get home, take a shower, and then head to the office. Thomas's attorney filed a motion to dismiss this morning. Hannah and I have drafted a response, but I need to file it with the court before the hearing this morning."

She undid the apron and hung it on a hook next to the refrigerator. "Just plate the burritos when Hannah comes down. Make sure she eats, will you? She gets stressed and forgets."

"Yes, ma'am." Ryker placed a kiss on the older woman's cheek. Pam was a local, and while she'd lived in different places over the years, had maintained close ties to the town. She'd known Ryker since he was in diapers and was close to his mother. "Don't worry. I'll take good care of your girls."

She patted his shoulder. "I know you will. See you later."

With a last wave, she left. Silence descended in the kitchen. He took a moment to check his email for any updates on the case, and while progress had been made, the culprit was still at large. He guzzled coffee while eating a breakfast burrito. The food and caffeine went a long way to erasing his fatigue.

Footsteps on the staircase proceeded Hannah into the kitchen. She was dressed for work in a suit, her shiny hair pulled back into a professional bun. A few strands had wriggled loose and played with the delicate curves of her face. Light makeup added color to her cheeks, but nothing could erase the faint circles under her eyes. She hadn't slept well. In her arms, she carried Charlotte.

Ryker's heart inexplicably kicked up a notch. The woman was stunning, and the sight of her holding the baby, conjured up white picket fences and puppies. His reaction was disconcerting. Hannah wasn't the kind of woman who'd entertain a casual relationship, and he had no intention of settling down.

Losing his first love in a tragic and sudden way had impacted his heart deeply. He couldn't imagine how painful it would be to lose a spouse. Ryker had decided a long time ago he didn't want to risk finding out. Until now, there'd never been a reason to question that decision. But this attraction to Hannah was unlike anything he'd ever experienced before. It was deep and powerful and visceral.

"Morning." Determined to keep things casual, Ryker set his mug on the counter. "Pam made breakfast burritos. I hope you're hungry. There's fresh coffee too."

"Wow." Hannah arched her brows as she settled Charlotte into a highchair and strapped her in. Her gaze swept across the table, which held a fruit salad and glasses of orange juice. "She didn't need to go to all this trouble. My normal breakfast is an apple as I slide out the door. Where is Pam anyway?"

"She left for the office." Ryker scooped up scrambled eggs seasoned with peppers, tomatoes, sausage, and cheese with a spatula. A warm tortilla rested nearby on a plate. He added the eggs and set it on the table before tilting his head toward the television playing quietly in the corner. A news reporter was standing outside Hannah's neighborhood, microphone in hand, giving the latest on the attack. "You'll need more than an apple to get through the morning. Someone leaked the contents of the letter to the media sometime last night."

Hannah's nose wrinkled. "I know. My boss called me early this morning. Thomas's attorney, Jose Ortiz, has filed a motion to dismiss. It's on the docket for later this morning. They're hoping to get the case thrown out by the judge."

Ryker wasn't surprised. In fact, he wouldn't put it past Jose to have leaked the letter himself. The defense attorney was known for playing dirty and doing whatever it took to get his clients off. As a result, he was paid top dollar by drug dealers, killers, and white-collar criminals. "Do you think the judge will throw the case out?"

"No, but I'm going to face more pressure to let this case go."

"From who? Not your boss, right?"

Hannah worked for the District Attorney, Bruce Foster, who'd been elected last year. He'd accepted campaign contributions from Thomas. As a result, he'd recused himself from handling any aspect of the case in order to appear impartial. The decision was smart politically, but it put Hannah in a vulnerable position.

"No, Bruce won't interfere with my decisions. He's escaped a lot of heat by recusing himself." She crossed to the pantry and removed a jar of baby food. "But the constant media coverage means that someone's head is going to roll if things don't go well. Since I'm in charge of pursuing this case—"

"You'll be the one to take the blame."

She nodded. Ryker's chest tightened at the stress riding the narrow line of her shoulders. Hannah wouldn't lose her job if she didn't nail a conviction, but she could be demoted. Or moved to a different department. Coupled with the threats on her life and caring for her niece... it was a lot for anyone to take on. He took the jar of baby food from her hand. "I'll feed Charlotte since I've already eaten. Dig in before your food gets cold."

Hannah hesitated, eyeing him suspiciously.

Ryker pulled out a chair next to the baby. "Don't look at me like that. I've got a big family with scads of little ones always running around. When it comes to feeding kids, I'm a pro." He gently tweaked Charlotte's dimpled chin, which earned him a gummy smile. "We're gonna be fine, aren't we, darlin'?" Then he smiled charmingly in Hannah's direction. "Word of warning, I don't do diapers."

That comment earned him a laugh. "Got it." She settled into a chair. Her head bowed and a silent prayer moved her lips before she dug into her breakfast burrito. Her eyes widened after taking the first bite. "This is so good. I didn't know Pam cooked this well. She's been keeping secrets."

Ryker laughed. "You should get her to bake you some Snickerdoodles. They're fantastic."

"Good to know."

He scooped baby food onto a plastic spoon and offered it to Charlotte. She obligingly opened her mouth. Little fists banged in excitement on the high chair tray. "Were you able to get hold of your brother or sister-in-law last night?"

"I sent them an email explaining that everything is okay." Fire flashed in her eyes. "Normally I wouldn't say anything since they're in war zones. Distraction can get them killed. But since the media picked up the story, I can't be sure they won't hear about it somehow. Ben and Danielle are going to be worried sick. I hope my email convinces them it's all under control." She grimaced and set down her burrito. "It's bad enough Charlotte was here during the break-in. I've said half a dozen prayers thanking God for keeping her safe."

He understood exactly what she was feeling. Ryker had spent the early-morning hours in prayer as well. "I know you're concerned about distracting them with the news, but it's better to hear it from you than the media."

"Pam said the same thing. We also discussed what to do with Charlotte this morning. Normally she goes to daycare, but I don't feel comfortable being separated from her after what happened last night, so Pam will watch her while I'm in court." Hannah sighed. "It's not professional to take Charlotte to work with me, but given the circumstances, I want her behind metal detectors in a place with a large police presence."

It was a smart move. Hannah's office was on the second floor of the courthouse. Access was restricted to personnel with badges and visitors had to be escorted through the area. Additionally, deputies guarded the main entrance to the courthouse, as well as the courtrooms, so there were always a dozen or more on duty at all times. Charlotte should be safe.

"Have you heard anything from Claire?" Hannah lifted the coffee mug to her lips. "Or anyone else on the ranger team? I know it's only been a few hours, but the sooner we catch the perpetrator, the better."

Ryker gently wiped the baby's mouth with a napkin. "There were no fingerprints on the note, on the knife the perpetrator took from you, or around the access point he used to gain entrance to the house."

"Not surprising. He was wearing gloves."

He nodded. "None of your neighbors saw anything. Some of them have cameras pointed toward the street, but there wasn't anything suspicious on them, which leads us to believe the perpetrator snuck in through the woods adjacent to your backyard. From what we can tell, he used an illegal jammer to mess with your security system. They're shockingly easy to buy on the dark web."

"So we're likely dealing with someone who's broken into houses before. This isn't an amateur or a newbie." Worry creased her brow. "That's frightening."

It was. "Claire is comparing the attacker's note to the

other death threats you've received in the last few months."

"Good. I don't want to assume Thomas is behind this when it could be someone else. The case has been in the news for months. Nothing the intruder said in the letter shows an intimate knowledge of Julie's murder. We could be dealing with some kind of copycat looking to get my attention."

Ryker understood where Hannah was coming from, but he wasn't buying it. Thomas had the most to gain from last night's attack and was already using the note to his advantage. He had to be behind this. Still, as a member of law enforcement, Ryker vowed to follow the evidence. They needed to track down every lead.

"What about the DNA?" Hannah asked.

"The lab is rushing it, but they'll need a few days." He met her gaze. "We're going to find this guy, Hannah. I promise you. Until then, you and I will stick together 24/7 until the perpetrator is caught."

Her brows arched. "24/7? Is that necessary? I know you have a life. Claire can set up extra patrols—"

"No." Ryker's tone brooked no argument. "Nothing is more important than keeping you and Charlotte safe."

Her eyes widened with the force of his words and Ryker sucked in a breath to temper his tone. He didn't want to think or acknowledge how much emotion had been buried in that statement. He'd kept his feelings for Hannah under lock and key for a long time. It needed to stay that way.

He scraped the last of the baby food from the jar. "Of

course, the level of protection is entirely up to you. If you don't want me involved, then that's your choice. But I hope you decide otherwise."

She studied him with that intense gaze of hers. Searching his expression as if trying to make sense of him. Ryker forced himself to maintain a casual posture while feeding the last bite to Charlotte. Maybe he was overreacting, and the threat was over. He prayed that was the case. But deep down, Ryker didn't believe it.

He feared things were just beginning.

FIVE

It took coordination and several deputies, along with Ryker, to sneak Hannah and Charlotte into the Fulton County Courthouse. She breathed a sigh of relief as the elevator doors opened on the second floor. Cubicles for support staff made up the center of the room while offices lined the outer wall.

Pam was waiting for them. Hannah's paralegal was loyal, whip-smart, and talented. Her tightly curled gray hair and crystal glasses gave her a grandmotherly appearance that was deceptively soft. Pam could be your best friend, but if you crossed her or someone she cared about, there was serious trouble.

She hustled them into Hannah's office and shut the door. "The hearing is set for ten this morning. I've filed the response with the clerk, so everything is ready to go." Pam extended her hands for Charlotte. "Come to me, sweetie. We're gonna spend a little time together while your auntie fights the bad guys."

Charlotte went willingly to Pam. She smiled and reached for the dangly earring hanging from the older woman's earlobes. Pam deftly removed the jewelry before tucking it into her pocket. "Silly me. I should've taken those off before you arrived." She tickled the little girl. Charlotte released a peel of laughter, which brought a smile to Hannah's face.

Ryker set the diaper bag down on a visitor's chair. "That thing weighs a ton. How much can one baby need?"

Hannah chuckled. "You'd be surprised." She turned back to Pam. "You've got diapers and formula and toys. She's teething, so I put a couple of frozen rings in the cooler along with a few ready-made bottles."

Pam waved a hand dismissively. "We'll be fine."

A knock came on the office door. Hannah spotted her boss, Bruce, through the glass cutout in the wood. She waved for him to enter.

Bruce swung the door wide. His suit was designer and tailored to fit his lean frame. Thinning gray hair was brushed away from his face and glasses gave him a distinctive air. He was smart, politically malleable, and expedient.

Behind him was Kristin Carmichael. A fellow assistant district attorney, she'd quickly climbed the ranks by proving herself valuable, but she lacked the courtroom experience and dedication to details that would turn her from a good lawyer into a great one. Hannah had been mentoring her for a while. With little success. Kristin often insisted on doing things her own way.

Bruce shut the door behind him and his gaze swept the room. Hannah introduced Ryker. Her boss acknowledged him with a polite nod, but Kristin flashed him a man-eating smile before extending her hand for him to shake. To Ryker's credit, he kept their interaction professional and brief.

"May I have a word with you, ADA Lawson?" Bruce tilted his head toward the far side of the room.

Hannah nodded and led the way. The angle provided some privacy from the rest of the people in the office, and by keeping their voices low, the conversation would remain private.

"Sorry to interrupt before the hearing," Bruce said. "But I got your email regarding the latest developments in the case. I'm troubled by the allegation that Thomas is behind this. In order to keep things on track, I'm assigning Kristin as second chair. She can assist with witness prep and take over questioning in court if need be."

Shock vibrated through Hannah. Bruce had never assigned another lawyer to one of her cases before without asking first. "If you're worried about my abilities, sir, I can assure you last night's attack—"

He held up a hand to ward off her words. "That's not it at all. I don't doubt you one bit. But this case is turning into a media frenzy. Since Thomas was a campaign donor, I can't be seen interfering, but I don't want you to be the sole face of this trial either. Kristin has proven herself adept at handling high-profile cases in the past.

She knows how to get the job done, thanks to your strong mentoring."

Hannah weighed her reply. Yes, Kristin was an accomplished lawyer, but she was also hungry for fame. "I appreciate the support, sir, but I don't want there to be any confusion about who is calling the shots."

"There won't be. You do. Kristin is second-chair only." Bruce lowered his hand to Hannah's shoulder and gave it a squeeze. "This is a good thing. I want you to bail if the threats become too much. You're caring for Charlotte now. There's more on your plate than just work. If things get to be too much, you can back out, and Kristin can take over as first-chair."

Ahhhh, and there it was. Hannah felt a surge of irritation. She had the sense Kristin had gone straight into Bruce's office with a plan to get on this case. And it'd worked.

Hannah calculated her next words carefully. "Sir, if you would like to assign a second-chair, I'm fine with that. But Kristin is too valuable to spend her time in witness prep. Larry would be a better choice. Or Nancy."

"Their dockets are full." He puffed out his chest and hooked the button to close his suit jacket. "Kristin closed a high-level case last night with a plea bargain. All of her other trials are weeks away. Plus, she's a fantastic lawyer, which you'll need."

His mind was made up. Hannah let out the breath she was holding. "Of course. Thank you, sir."

Bruce nodded and led the way out of the alcove. He said goodbye to everyone before turning back to Hannah.

"Keep me updated. And good luck in the hearing this morning."

She nodded, and he left. Pam was digging through the diaper bag while Kristin and Ryker were standing together having a low conversation. The younger lawyer placed a hand on his arm and laughed, throwing her head back as if he'd said the funniest thing in the world. Ryker glanced at Hannah and then his gaze skirted away. A sinking suspicion settled in her stomach. She approached the couple.

Kristin smiled saccharinely in Hannah's direction. "I'm excited to join the team. This case is fascinating, and it's rare something this big happens in a county of this size." She finally dropped her hand from Ryker's arm. "I borrowed the case files to review. Hope you don't mind. It's the fastest way to get up to speed."

Hannah bit back her initial retort and sent up a prayer for patience. She suspected Kristin had maneuvered her way onto the case, but didn't have proof. There was no sense in making their working relationship contentious. At the same time, Hannah had no intention of having her authority challenged. "I'm sure Bruce has made you aware, but just in case he hasn't, you're second chair. All strategy decisions or issues need to be run by me."

"Absolutely."

She met and held the other woman's gaze. Kristin was ambitious, and her desire for attention could wreak havoc if she "accidentally" let something slip to the media. "As I'm sure you are aware, there is a gag order in place regarding this case. You cannot speak to the media about any aspect, nor can you discuss it with anyone in the office who isn't assigned to work on it."

The judge had ordered the measure after Thomas's media blitz. Unfortunately, damage had been done. He'd convinced members of the community that he was innocent of murdering his wife, which fueled speculation about Julie's killer.

Kristin nodded, placing her finger over her lips. "No one will hear anything from me."

"Good. Then I'll see you in the courtroom. Welcome to the team."

"Thanks."

With a last flirty smile in Ryker's direction, Kristin slipped from the office.

Pam scowled. "That woman maneuvered her way onto this case by convincing Bruce it was the right thing to do. She's ambitious." The older woman hiked Charlotte up higher on her hip. "Watch yourself with that one, Hannah. There are rumors running around the office that she's jealous of the cases you've been getting."

Her paralegal's observations mirrored Hannah's own, but she had bigger issues than a competing attorney. She stuffed a writing pad into her laptop bag. "I can handle Kristin." She glanced at her watch. "But if I don't hurry, I'll be late to court and Judge Wingate will have my hide."

Pam handed her a copy of their reply to the defense's motion. "Good luck."

"Thanks." She took the paperwork and added it to

her laptop bag before kissing Charlotte goodbye. Ryker fell into step beside her as they hurried down the hall. Hannah mentally debated asking the question, lingering on the tip of her tongue. The issue was personal, and normally would be none of her business, but now... it had to be handled. Especially if Ryker was going to be acting as her protection detail. The last thing Hannah needed was more surprises.

She waited until they were in the elevator before rounding to face him. "Are you and Kristin dating?"

SIX

It wasn't often Ryker was left speechless, but Hannah's question had come out of left field. He stared at her, incredulous. "No, I'm not dating Kristin."

Her gaze narrowed. "Have you ever dated her? Actually, have you ever dated someone from my office that is working on this case?"

"I have no idea." He couldn't possibly know every staff member assigned to the case. A murder trial this big potentially had several paralegals and other support staff working under Hannah. "Is it a problem if I've dated someone from your office?"

"It could be if you're distracted." Her eyes flashed with some indescribable emotion. "Let's not play games. You have a reputation, Ryker. You're known as a flirt, and I have the sense you're seen as a challenge. There's a particular woman that enjoys that game. From the looks of things in my office, Kristin is one of them. And I don't need that kind of distraction on top of everything else."

The elevator dinged, and the doors swished open. Hannah bolted out and Ryker had to double-time it to catch up to her. He lightly snagged her elbow to slow her steps. Aware there were people around, he steered Hannah into a small alcove off a courtroom. This conversation wasn't over.

He kept his voice pitched low. "I told you this morning, nothing is more important than keeping you and Charlotte safe." For a moment, Ryker nearly told her about losing Alison. His whole life changed in an instant, and he'd never risk adding more guilt to his shoulders by failing to protect Hannah. But now was not the time or the place to share that story. Instead, he merely said, "Kristin and I have never dated. Nor will we."

"Why not? She's smart and beautiful. Seems like she'd be your type."

Ryker was starting to believe his type was fiery redheads, but wisely kept that comment to himself. "Despite my reputation"—he used air quotes around reputation—"I've only dated a few women in the last several years. I flirt, yes, but that's as far as it goes."

She jutted up her chin. "Even that can be an issue."

"True, but despite what you may have heard, I have a sense of time and place. I don't walk around flirting indiscriminately."

"Have you noticed the way your smile affects women? Seems pretty indiscriminate to me."

She sounded annoyed, and Ryker briefly wondered if Hannah was jealous, but that was out of character for her and their relationship. He shoved the thought aside as quickly as it formed. "So smiling is off the table too?"

"No." She closed her eyes and breathed out. Guilt flickered across her features. "I'm sorry. The question was out of line. It implied you couldn't keep things professional. That's not a fair assertion."

"No, but I understand why you were concerned." He placed a hand lightly on her forearm. The scent of her perfume—something light and flowery—filled his senses, distracting him momentarily with its enticing fragrance. Heaven help him, the only woman who might serve as a distraction was Hannah herself. "For the record, again, I have only dated a handful of women from the court-house. All of those relationships were casual. We parted as friends. None of those relationships should cause an issue, even if they are working on this case."

She bit her lip and nodded. "Okay." Hannah glanced at the hallway behind him. "We'd better go. There's Thomas and his attorney."

Hannah did her best to compartmentalize the conversation with Ryker to the back of her mind as they continued down the hallway to the courtroom. She peeked at him out of the corner of her eye. He'd handled her question with grace and compassion, which was probably more than she deserved considering the ambush in the elevator. Her concerns might've been valid, but she hadn't handled them well.

She didn't want to think that jealousy might've fueled her response. That was ridiculous. Ryker had never shown the least bit of interest in her. Never flirted with her once. And she didn't want him to. Except... except she could still feel the warmth of his palm on her arm even though he'd stopped touching her. It'd practically seared itself into her skin through the fabric of her suit.

It was unsettling. Hannah hadn't even looked at a man twice since her husband died. This attraction to Ryker was ill advised. She needed to get it under control before feelings developed.

Reporters gathered outside the courtroom spotted Hannah approaching and headed straight for her like a mass of swarming bees. Claustrophobia threatened as they pressed around screaming rapid-fire questions she couldn't answer thanks to the gag order. She hated this.

Ryker placed a steadying hand on the small of her back. His solid presence grounded her as she moved through the throng until they reached the ornate wooden doors where deputies pushed back the crowd to allow entrance into the courtroom. Several more journalists were already seated inside, but per the judge's rules, didn't move to ask questions. Some of them had sketch pads. Cameras—thanks to another one of Judge Wingate's orders—weren't permitted in the courtroom.

Julie's mother, Mandy Jackson, stood near the railing separating the public area of the courtroom from the judge's bench. She twisted a set of tissues in her hand and glared at her former son-in-law who was seated with his lawyer at the defense table. In her other hand, Mandy held two visible photographs. One was of Julie. Her daughter had been a vibrant and beautiful thirty-year-old with a wide smile and sparkling brown eyes. The other picture was a sonogram. The only one taken of Julie's unborn baby. She'd been eight weeks pregnant at the time of her murder.

Hannah shared a glance with Ryker and headed straight for the older woman. "Mandy, you didn't need to come to this hearing."

"Hannah." Mandy hugged her briefly. "Of course I did. I made a promise to come to everything. For Julie's sake."

"I know you miss her very much." Ryker's tone was compassionate.

"I'm angry, if you want to know the truth." Mandy sniffed and wiped at her nose. Her eyes were red-rimmed, as if she'd spent the morning crying. "I couldn't believe it when I saw someone had broken into your house, Hannah, and attacked you. Then when the journalists talked about that note..." Her expression hardened. "This is Thomas's doing. He's trying to wriggle out of being convicted. Please tell me you're going to fight for my daughter."

This was one of the hardest parts of Hannah's job. Dealing with grieving family members who rightly wanted justice took a delicate hand. So much of what happened in the courtroom was out of her control, and there were no guarantees. She was careful not to make false promises. "I'm going to do everything I can for Julie,

Mrs. Jackson. Ultimately, it's the judge—or the jury, if we get that far—who makes the final decision." She smiled gently. "But I'm not a quitter. You can count on that."

"Thank you." The older woman blotted her eyes with the crumpled tissues.

Ryker gestured to a nearby bench. "Come with me, Mrs. Jackson. We'll sit together."

Hannah shot him a grateful glance before slipping through the swinging door to the prosecution table. Kristin was already there, laptop open and court documents arranged neatly. She crooked a finger to indicate Hannah should lean closer.

"What are the chances Thomas will win this motion to dismiss?" Kristin asked.

"Not high, but I don't think that's the end goal." Hannah removed a copy of the letter left at her home. The original had been taken into evidence. "His attorney wants to get this admitted into evidence at the trial. It supports the theory that Thomas was approached by a drug dealer to write illegal narcotic prescriptions, and when he refused, his wife was killed in retaliation. Has Jose given you an additional motion?"

"No, but he's heading this way with something in his hand."

Hannah glanced up to find Thomas's attorney, Jose Ortiz, approaching their table. He wore an expensive three-piece suit, his hair cut sharply away from patrician features. As expected, he slid a motion in front of her. "One more small matter we intend to bring up today with the judge."

She scanned it. As expected, the motion requested the judge allow the letter into evidence. "I'm going to object."

He shrugged and picked an invisible piece of lint from his jacket. "Then we'll see how the judge rules." He shot her a cocky smile. "Come on, Hannah. You can't possibly win this case. Drop the charges and let's all go home."

"Not a chance." She glanced over at the defense table. Thomas was staring at her. Nearing thirty-five, he had the healthy good looks of a man who spent a lot of time outdoors and the physique of a swimmer. He was under house arrest, so he hadn't been able to work, but his sprawling estate comprised fifteen acres. It had horses, a swimming pool, and a tennis court.

Thomas met Hannah's gaze. A smirk played on his lips, but his eyes were cold. Flat. She could easily imagine him stabbing his wife to death.

She turned her attention back to Jose. "The break-in at my house and the appearance of this note is suspect. If I find out your client had anything to do with it, I will throw every single charge I can at him and fight to get him the harshest sentence possible."

"That's a horrible accusation." Jose's expression twisted into mock outrage. "Of course Thomas had nothing to do with this. He's not a killer."

That had yet to be determined. Hannah arched her brows. "I hope you're right."

Jose's face flushed. "You're playing a dangerous game. Thomas has lost his wife and unborn baby, been arrested and charged with their murders, had his good name dragged through the mud, and was ignored at every turn when he told the police about the drug dealer, Cash. Now you want to accuse him of arranging an attack on you. That's... beyond the pale." He leaned closer. "If you continue with this, it'll go badly for you. Very badly."

A shiver of fear worked its way down her spine. Jose was known for fighting hard for his clients, and he represented an unsavory bunch, but he'd never done anything untoward.

Until now.

It took everything in Hannah to maintain eye contact. "That sounds like a threat."

His gaze narrowed. "It's an observation. The DA, your boss, doesn't like to have egg on his face. If you lose this case, which you will, it'll end badly for you."

"Thanks for your concern, but I can handle my career." Hannah found his behavior incredibly odd. A sneaking suspicion crept into the recesses of her mind. Did Jose know his client was guilty? Of murdering his wife and arranging the attack on Hannah? It was possible. Most defense attorneys never asked their clients directly about guilt or innocence. There were a lot of reasons for that. But Jose didn't strike her as the kind who would shy away from a case even if he knew his client was guilty.

It was also possible he was just feeling the pressure. Given the media's attention, it would be a huge bonus if Jose won this case. It would bring in more clients who'd pay top-dollar for a successful defense attorney. Then again, he could spin a loss into something profitable too.

Their conversation was cut off when the bailiff announced the judge. Jose hurried back to his table as Judge Wingate entered, robes billowing, and climbed the dais before taking her seat. Nerves jittered in Hannah's stomach as the judge announced the case for the record. Ryker caught her eye, his gaze shooting toward Jose and then back to her, a question written in his raised brows. Clearly, he'd caught the exchange and found it as odd as she had. Hannah shook her head to show she was all right and turned her attention back to the matter at hand: winning this hearing.

She and Jose battled for over twenty minutes. The result was that his motion to dismiss was denied. The trial would move forward next week as planned. However, the judge delayed ruling on whether to admit the letter left at Hannah's house into evidence. Not a loss, exactly, but it was cause for concern. She couldn't let the letter be presented to the jury. It would create reasonable doubt, which is exactly what Thomas was counting on.

Once the hearing was over, she turned to Kristin. "We need to find precedent. I doubt you'll find a case with a similar fact pattern, but see if there's something close. I need to give the judge a reason to keep this letter away from the jury." Hannah breathed out. "I can't cross-exam a note. That might be a good place to start."

The younger woman scribbled some notes. "On it."

Some of the tension riding Hannah's shoulders eased. Kristin was ambitious, but there was a way to harness that power for good. She was an excellent researcher. Tenacious. She wouldn't stop until she'd found something to help win the argument.

Ryker appeared by her side. "You did it." His expression was infused with warmth. "You kept the charges against Thomas from being dropped and the letter out of evidence."

"I bought us some time, that's all. Unless we can conclusively prove Thomas hired someone to attack me, then Judge Wingate will probably allow the letter into evidence during the trial. She won't risk an innocent man going to prison."

Hannah's attention drifted across the courtroom to the defense table. Thomas and his lawyer were speaking together in low voices. Both of them were grinning like they'd won the lottery. Maybe this letter had dropped from the heavens like a gift from God, but Hannah didn't think so. She was buying into Ryker's theory more and more. Thomas had hired someone to attack her.

The real question was who?

Sudden movement caught Hannah's attention as the bailiff hung up his cell phone and raced to the judge's bench. He whispered something in her ear.

Judge Wingate stiffened and then rose. "Excuse me, ladies and gentlemen, we need to evacuate the building immediately. There's been a bomb threat."

SEVEN

Ryker's heart leapt to his throat as he grabbed Hannah's elbow. "We've got to go. Now."

The bailiff hurried across the courtroom and yanked on the fire alarm. A siren immediately started blaring. Kristin paled and jumped up. She pointed to the exit. "The fastest way out of the building is over there."

"No." Hannah yanked out of Ryker's hold. "I'm not going anywhere without Charlotte."

Before he could respond, the stubborn woman spun on her heel and hurried for the door leading to the interior of the courthouse and her office. Ryker had no choice but to follow her. Frustration swelled in his chest as he scrambled to make it through the door and past the swaths of people moving toward the exit. It was like swimming upstream. Several bailiffs were trying to keep the crowd calm, but to no avail. Panic was setting in. A woman tripped and Ryker's hand shot out to steady her before pushing forward.

"Hannah!" He finally caught up to her and grabbed her arm. The sheer worry etched on her pretty features cut him to the core. Charlotte wasn't Hannah's daughter, but the love she had for her niece ran strong.

And heaven help him, Ryker admired her deeply for it.

"This way." He'd studied the schematics for the courthouse last night. There was a shortcut through another set of offices. Ryker tugged Hannah through a side door into an empty hallway. One hand held hers, the softness of her palm noticeable even with the trouble facing them. His other hand was on his holstered weapon. Ryker wasn't sure if a bomb had actually been planted in the courthouse or if the phone call was a diversion. Either way, one thing was obvious. Hannah was in danger. She was the target. Ryker needed to get her—and Charlotte—out of here as fast as possible.

Had the attacker gone after the baby? It was possible. The thought sent Ryker's heart rate into higher gear and quickened his steps. There was no denying the fastest way to hurt Hannah would be to threaten her niece. The intruder last night had ignored Charlotte, thank God, but it would be arrogant to assume he would continue to do so. Ryker mentally berated himself for not leaving a bailiff stationed outside Hannah's office.

He would never forgive himself if something happened to Charlotte.

The fire alarm continued to blare as they hurried for the rear of the building through a network of interconnecting hallways. Ryker took the stairs to the upper floor two at a time. Finally, they were deposited in the right area. Cubicles for support staff and paralegals gathered in the center of the large space. The door to Hannah's office came into view. It was open. She raced for it, running faster in high heels than Ryker could've imagined possible.

"Pam!" Hannah's voice carried. She went into the office and turned in a circle. "She's gone."

"They must've already evacuated." Ryker realized the diaper bag was also missing. "We'll find them. Come on."

He grabbed Hannah's hand again and tugged her out of the office. Movement in his periphery caught his attention. Ryker whirled around just as Pam's head popped out from an adjacent cubicle. She held Charlotte in her arms. Relief washed over him, but was quickly replaced by concern as he registered the look of panic on the older woman's face. She caught sight of them and bit back a sob.

Hannah raced forward. "What happened? Are you hurt?" She plucked the baby from Pam's arms. Charlotte was crying, her face red. The baby appeared unharmed but was bothered by the blare of the alarm. Hannah pressed her little head against her chest and cupped a hand over Charlotte's other tiny ear.

"Mrs. Pam." Ryker placed a hand under the paralegal's elbow. He noticed one of her shoes was across the aisle. Her previously styled hair was a mess and her pantyhose were ripped at the knees. "Are you injured?"

"It's my foot. Someone pushed me as we were leaving

the office and I fell." She swiped at the tears on her face. "I forgot my cell in Hannah's office and couldn't figure out how to get back while carrying the baby. Thank goodness you came back for us." She lifted a hand to her hair. "I also whacked my head on something when I fell."

Ryker quickly assessed Pam's injury. Her ankle was swollen and tender to the touch. Possibly broken. More concerning was the large lump forming on the back of her skull near her nape. Her pupils were dilated. Concussion.

Why hadn't anyone helped her? Panic, created by the alarms and the bomb threat, had created a mob mentality. He hesitated, uncertainty swirling inside him. Carrying Pam would prevent him from being able to draw his weapon, but considering there was a bomb threat, paramedics wouldn't be able to enter until everything was secure. And what happened if the threat wasn't an empty one? There legitimately could be a bomb in the building.

They needed to get out of there. All of them.

"I'm going to carry you, Mrs. Pam." Ryker bent over and lifted the older woman into his arms. "Hannah, you and Charlotte follow behind me. Stay close, understand?"

He met her gaze for a moment. Every worry and concern flickering through his mind was reflected in her brilliant blue eyes. Then her jaw tightened with determination. Hannah nodded. "Let's go."

Ryker tightened his hold on Pam. Mindful of the older woman's injury, he carefully weaved his way through the cubicles to the staircase. His gaze never stopped moving, searching for potential trouble. Some internal instinct warned him that the danger was far from over. The sound of his cowboy boots and Hannah's heels reverberated off the concrete walls of the staircase. When they reached the lower floor, he led the way toward the closest exit. A swarm of people stampeded out of the courthouse. They'd packed one exit when others were clearly marked.

Ryker shouted to be heard over the din. "This way, people! There's more than one way out!"

Pam's skin was clammy. She was pale and her breathing was shallow. Ryker feared the older woman was going into shock. "Take deep breaths. I know you're frightened, but everything is going to be okay."

She needed a paramedic. He glanced behind him to check on Hannah. She was clutching Charlotte close, keeping a hand over the baby's ear to protect it from the screaming fire alarm. The little one had stopped crying. Her eyes were wide with fear though. Hannah's too, although she was doing an excellent job of funneling that emotion into keeping pace with Ryker.

A bang sounded down the hall and screams filled the space. Several people diverted toward the exit Ryker was also heading for. He tried to keep Pam's foot from being crushed in the bedlam. The double doors swung open wide as people pushed their way out. Sunshine hit Ryker in the face, momentarily blinding him. He hurried across the street toward first responders. A set of paramedics saw him coming and rushed to help Pam. They loaded her onto a gurney.

Ryker turned to check on Hannah. His heart skittered as his gaze flew over the immediate surroundings. Panic set in. He grabbed a man who'd been with them near the exit. "Did you see a woman and a baby?"

"No."

Several more people responded the same way. Ryker raced back toward the building. Searching. His gaze skipped over every face, but none of them belonged to the red-headed beauty.

Hannah and Charlotte were gone.

EIGHT

How was this happening?

Hannah winced as the barrel of a gun jabbed her kidney. A strong hand gripped her arm, hard enough to leave a bruise, as her kidnapper steered her away from the crowd. Fear and adrenaline narrowed her vision to the empty hallway ahead. Charlotte was nestled against her. With one ear pressed against Hannah's chest and the other protected by her hand, the wailing fire alarm was muffled. The poor little lamb had fallen asleep, tuckered out after her screaming spell earlier.

One moment they'd been following behind Ryker and Pam. The next, she had a gun shoved in her back. The attacker's whispered words replayed in her mind.

Scream and I'll shoot you. Then anyone who tries to help you.

He meant it. Hannah couldn't risk Charlotte's life. Or anyone else's, for that matter. Nor could she fight off an attacker while carrying a baby. So she'd obeyed.

Where he was leading her, she didn't know. Hannah tried to glance over her shoulder at the attacker. "Please, don't do this."

"Shut up." His voice was hard. "Keep moving."

She dragged her feet, hoping to slow him down long enough for Ryker to realize they were missing. How long would it take? The Texas Ranger would come for them, but given the bomb threat, he might be prevented from re-entering the building until it was secure. "The police will look for me. I'm an Assistant District Attorney. That makes me an officer of the law. Kidnapping me is a felony."

"I said shut up!"

His grip on her arm tightened until it felt like he was grinding her bone. Hannah muffled a scream fueled by pain and terror. Tears pricked her eyes. It took every ounce of strength inside her to wrestle them back. Now was not the time to fall apart. Not while Charlotte was in danger. Whatever came next, Hannah had to keep a level head in order to protect her niece.

No one was going to hurt Charlotte. No one.

It was unimaginable that only a few months ago Hannah had fretted over becoming her niece's temporary guardian. She read baby books, joined parenting groups online, and talked to other mothers in the DA's office. The responsibility of caring for the little girl wasn't something she took lightly and, ultimately, Hannah worried that she'd be incapable of providing the love that Charlotte needed. Prayer had been the way through those fears. It would be her way through this too.

Heavenly Father, give me the guidance I need to protect Charlotte. Help me find a way out of this. In You I trust.

The petition eased some of Hannah's terror as they entered the open doors to the courthouse cafeteria. Chairs were overturned, half-eaten meals forgotten in the rush to escape the building. Someone had spilled coffee. The lid rested on the floor next to some of the dark liquid. The rest of the drink coated the table.

No one was there. Hannah had no ability to signal anyone for help.

She glanced over her shoulder again at the man as he forced her toward the rear of the cafeteria. His blond hair was stringy and long, some of it hanging in his meaty face. She cataloged his features. Crooked nose. Thin lips and ruddy cheeks. A distinctive scar sliced his neck, as though not too long ago, he'd nearly had his throat slashed. Despite his rough appearance, he was dressed in nice clothing. Professional clothing. He could've passed for a defendant, a juror, or even a witness.

Nothing about him was familiar. Hannah didn't think their paths had ever crossed before. "Why are you doing this?" She took a gamble. "Money?"

He growled in response and kept shoving her forward. They were heading toward a service exit. Did he have a vehicle waiting? This side of the building faced an alley that was used for delivering supplies. Hannah dragged her feet more. The only thing more terrifying than being held at gunpoint was the prospect of leaving the building with this man. "Whatever you're being paid, I can double it."

That comment earned her a laugh, but he didn't refute her assertion that he'd been hired to kidnap her. Was this the same man who'd attacked her in her house last night? She believed so.

The intruder had ignored Charlotte after breaking into the house. An idea formed in her mind. Hannah swallowed hard as the delivery bay came into view. Sure enough, there was a white van waiting. The side door was open. She slowed her pace even more. "Wait, please. You want me, you don't want the baby. If I can leave her somewhere safe, then I'll get into the van without causing you any trouble."

He paused. Hannah, sensing she was on to something, added, "She's innocent. Please."

His gaze dropped to Charlotte, and then he growled again. He shoved Hannah toward a supply closet. "Put her in there. And make it snappy, or I'll lose my patience, and kill you both."

The threat sent Hannah's heart rate spiking. She nearly tripped in her hurry to deposit Charlotte some place safe. The interior of the closet was dim, the only light shining from the hallway. Paper towels, cleaning supplies, and boxes lined the shelves. Her attacker lurked in the doorway. His face was cast in shadow, but the gun was visible.

Hannah quickly located several clean towels used for wiping down tables. She tossed toilet paper out of a half-empty box and lined it with the soft fabric before laying a still-sleeping Charlotte into the makeshift bed. Her dark hair curled over one smooth cheek, and her lips made a sucking motion, before she sighed. Fearing it was the last time she'd see her precious little niece, Hannah captured every detail in her mind like a snapshot.

A rough hand grabbed her bicep. Hannah nearly toppled over in her heels as the attacker dragged her to a standing position. The gun was once again shoved into her side. She winced but stifled the terror threatening to overwhelm her senses. As he swung her toward the doorway, her gaze snagged on a set of tools.

She stumbled. Pain erupted through her body as Hannah fell into the shelving unit. Paper towels toppled from the top rack, bouncing against the concrete floor. Her hand brushed against something sharp. She wrapped her fingers around the metal object.

A screwdriver.

Thank you, Lord.

The attacker forcefully yanked Hannah to her feet. Sweat beaded on her back as he pulled her from the closet into the delivery bay. The air was heavy with the scent of more rain. Heart pounding and chest tight, she maneuvered the screwdriver against her leg until her fingers gripped the handle. The weapon was poor defense against a gun, but it was something. It was a fighting chance.

"How are you going to get out of here?" She needed a distraction. One moment when he dropped the gun away from her body. "The courthouse is surrounded by police. They won't let you pass."

"Let me worry about that." The gun barrel hit her kidney again. "Pick up the pace."

"Police!" Ryker's voice vibrated off the concrete walls of the delivery bay. "Drop your weapon!"

Still holding onto Hannah, the attacker retreated to a stack of boxes before whirling and pointing his gun at the Texas Ranger.

"No!" Hannah shoved him with all her might.

He pitched forward. She let her body go limp, forcing the gunman to release her. The concrete was cold against her skin. Hannah gripped the screwdriver and raised her arm. Without thinking, she stabbed the attacker in the calf with her makeshift weapon.

He screamed.

She scrambled backward, desperate to put some distance between the gunman and her. Ryker's orders vibrated off the concrete and suddenly there was gunfire. Hannah's breathing grew shallow as she stayed low, hiding behind a collection of boxes. Her gaze searched the area for another weapon, but to no avail. Prayers fell from her lips. The sound of an engine rumbling to life was followed by more gunshots. Tires squealed. She caught sight of the van as it tore down the alley through large windows at the back of the bay.

The attacker had escaped.

She whimpered. Scrambling out of her hiding place, Hannah fell into a set of strong and capable arms. Ryker. His solid form held her up as her knees trembled. He pulled her closer until she was pressed against his muscular chest. "I've got you. It's okay. I've got you."

Tremors worked through her entire body. She wanted to bury herself in his embrace and forget about the last fifteen minutes, but couldn't. Hannah shoved away from Ryker. "Charlotte. She's in the storage closet." Bullets could tear through sheetrock. Fresh terror overtook her logic. She stumbled down the aisle of boxes, heading straight for her niece.

Was Charlotte okay?

NINE

Four hours later, Ryker's pulse still hadn't settled. The conference room in the Fulton County Sheriff's Department was a quiet oasis compared to the bullpen beyond the closed door. Hannah was seated on his right, Charlotte settled on her lap with a bottle. The baby was unharmed and blissfully unaware of the perilous danger she'd been in. Her cheeks were rosy as she sucked down the formula greedily. Every time Ryker glanced at her—or her gorgeous caregiver—his chest tightened.

They'd almost died.

Mistakes had been made. His own. Self-recrimination battered the confidence he'd built up over the years as a Texas Ranger. He'd been in precarious situations with civilians before—domestic violence, incidents with hostages—but all of them were instigated *before* his arrival on the scene. What happened today at the courthouse was his screw-up. And Hannah had nearly paid the ultimate price.

That wouldn't happen again. Not on his watch. He'd toss the woman over his shoulder and haul her out of danger next time if need be. His gaze drifted to the baby in her arms. Charlotte was another issue altogether. After this meeting, Ryker and Hannah were going to have a tough conversation. She had some decisions to make.

On the table, Hannah's phone buzzed with an incoming text. She scooped it up, read the message, and then her shoulders sagged with relief. "The hospital will keep Pam overnight for observation since she hit her head, but her ankle is just sprained." A new message came through, and Hannah chuckled. "Pam's daughter says her mom is arguing with the doctor because she wants to go home. Not even a knock to the head can keep her down."

Ryker laughed, relief loosening his muscles. He'd been worried about the older woman. "Sounds like she's gonna be just fine."

The conference room door opened and several members of his team, along with his boss, filed in. Introductions were made and more than one ranger went gooey-eyed over Charlotte. It was an interesting phenomenon to observe. Hardened lawmen with years of experience dealing with the worst criminals went completely soft over one small baby. Not that Ryker could blame them. Charlotte was completely adorable. She ate up all the attention, offering everyone a toothless smile, before Hannah convinced her to take the bottle again.

Claire, her sheriff's uniform wrinkled, marched in on

determined strides, followed by several of her deputies. She took a place at the center of the table and waved for everyone to have a seat. "Let's get started." She gave a sharp nod to Ryker's boss. "I'm turning this meeting over to Lieutenant Vikki Rodriguez. For those who aren't aware, she's in charge of Company A of the Texas Rangers. They are leading the investigation into the attacks on ADA Lawson and the bombing at the courthouse."

Texas Rangers couldn't assume control of a case without being invited to do so, and their investigations were often part of a larger task force in combination with local law enforcement. As sheriff, Claire was involved every step of the way. Joining their efforts was the most effective way to tackle tough cases.

Lieutenant Rodriguez rose from her chair. The leader of Company A was detail-oriented, tough, and kind. Ryker had always had a good working relationship with her. It helped that she treated her team like a family. The camaraderie in their unit was solid. While the lieutenant didn't let anyone on her team get away with nonsense, she also extended understanding when personal issues arose.

Her dark hair was slicked back into a tight ponytail and her makeup-free face was stern. "Thank you, Sheriff. This morning, the bailiff in Judge Wingate's courtroom received a call on his personal cell phone from an unidentified individual who claimed there was a bomb in the building. Understandably concerned, the bailiff alerted the judge and began an emergency evacuation of the building. The bomb squad—along with their canines—have been through every inch of the courthouse. No bombs were found.

"We believe the bomb threat was a well-timed ruse to create a panic in order to kidnap ADA Lawson," Lieutenant Rodriguez continued. "The perpetrator escaped in an unidentified van from the courthouse after exchanging gunfire with law enforcement. During his struggle with ADA Lawson, however, he was injured when she stabbed him with a screwdriver. Local hospitals have been notified, but there's no sign of him. Yet."

"Do we know if this perpetrator is the same man who attacked Hannah in her home last night?" Claire asked.

Texas Ranger Elijah "Eli" Goodwin, his usual permanent scowl etched on his features, leaned forward. "Not with certainty, although it's a safe bet. ADA Lawson fought off both attacks, drawing blood in the process. DNA will take time, but the blood type is a match. Either both attackers are AB- or we're dealing with the same man." Eli's scowl softened as he glanced at Hannah. A faint smile played on his lips. "Nice job, by the way. The screwdriver to the leg was a brilliant move. The guy's probably in a lot of pain. Is it wrong to hope the wound gets infected and forces him to a hospital so we can arrest his cowardly behind?"

A bolt of unexpected and white-hot jealousy streaked through Ryker. Eli was a childhood friend. They'd know each other for decades. Eli wasn't known for flirting. He hadn't so much as looked at a woman twice since breaking up with his fiancée five years ago. The man was as straitlaced as they came, a rule follower to a nauseating degree, and grumpy to boot. At any other time, Ryker would be amused to witness Eli so obviously intrigued by a woman. But not Hannah.

It was a ridiculous thought. One he had no right to. Hannah was free to date who she chose, and despite his critical attitude, she could do a lot worse than Eli. The ranger was loyal and went the extra mile with everything. Including caring for his friends. He'd bailed Ryker out of trouble many times over the years.

Still... Ryker was bothered. More than he wanted to admit. It didn't help when Hannah blushed slightly. He forced his mind to focus on the task at hand. "Whether his wound becomes infected or not, we're arresting his cowardly behind." A round of Amens followed that statement from the law enforcement in the room. Ryker waited until they died down before continuing, "The perpetrator left Hannah a note last night linking her assault to Julie Anderson's murder. If the courthouse attack was committed by the same man—and it probably was—this all links back to Thomas."

"The perpetrator alluded to being paid." Hannah patted the baby's back in rhythmic movements. "I offered to double the amount. He laughed in response."

"That's one possibility." Lieutenant Rodriguez nodded. "The perpetrator could be a hitman for hire. Someone Thomas Anderson contracted to kill you. But there's another plausible theory." She picked up a remote and clicked a button. An image of a man appeared on the far wall, courtesy of an overhead projector controlled by a laptop resting on the conference table. Ryker immediately recognized the kidnapper. His face was partially, although not completely, concealed by a ball cap.

"This photograph was taken from surveillance video at the courthouse," Lieutenant Rodriguez said. "We haven't been able to identify the perpetrator, but..." She clicked on the remote again. This time a side-by-side image appeared on the wall. One was the photograph of the attacker, the other was a police sketch artist rendering.

Hannah gasped. "That's the man Thomas said threatened him in his office parking lot. The one who he accused of killing his wife. Cash."

Ryker stiffened. She was right. There was a striking resemblance. The only differential was that the man from the courthouse had a large scar on his neck and the sketch did not. Tension coiled his muscles.

"It's possible Thomas Anderson was telling the truth," Lieutenant Rodriguez said. "He was approached by Cash with an offer to join forces in a drug scheme involving narcotics prescriptions. When Thomas refused, this man"—she pointed to the still photograph taken from the video surveillance—"retaliated by killing his wife."

Ryker gritted his teeth together. "We looked into Thomas's claims thoroughly and could never substantiate them. That composite sketch was done several weeks after Julie was murdered. That's when Thomas offered this supposed theory about his wife's death. At the time, he was already under suspicion. We were building a case against him, and he knew it."

From the grim looks on his fellow rangers' faces, they agreed with his assessment.

"I've read the reports, Ryker." His boss met his gaze. "No one—including you—did an insufficient job. However—" She gestured to the images. "We also can't ignore the evidence staring straight at us. The resemblance between Hannah's attacker and the composite sketch is obvious. It would be foolish to ignore the possibility that Cash murdered Julie."

"If that's true, why go after Hannah?" Eli asked.

"The killer left a note stating he wants acknowledgement for the murder." The lieutenant shrugged. "Hubris. Attention. A murderer's mind can be a confusing thing. We don't always understand why someone acts the way they do."

Texas Ranger Weston Donovan crossed his arms over his broad chest. The man was built like a tank. A former football star turned lawman, he'd lost none of his physical strength since retiring from the game. A wedding ring encased the third finger on his left hand. Weston was married to a university police chief. The couple were expecting their first child later in the year.

"I'm not buying it." Weston frowned. He'd assisted Ryker on the Anderson murder investigation and knew it well. "It seems very convenient that a killer shows up one week before Thomas's trial and leaves a note claiming responsibility for Julie's murder. How can we be sure Cash and Thomas didn't know each other before any of this went down?"

"We don't." Lieutenant Rodriguez planted her hands

on her hips. "Which is why we need to pursue every option and investigate every lead."

Hannah closed her eyes and sagged against her chair. She lifted a hand to her forehead and rubbed it as if a headache was gathering. "We don't have much time. Thomas's trial starts in a week. I could drop the charges against him and then file them again at a later date..." She lowered her hand. "But I doubt my boss will allow that. Given the media's attention, it's politically unwise for him to pursue this case a second time."

Frustration tangled inside Ryker. He understood the delicate position Hannah was in. Justice should be a straightforward matter, but often, politics and individual agendas got in the way. "What do you want to do?"

"I want the truth. The evidence against Thomas is strong, but that doesn't change the fact that the defense will use that man"—she gestured to the image of Cash on the wall—"against me in court. His attacks on me, along with the note, constitute reasonable doubt."

Ryker wanted to argue with her but couldn't. She was right. Doubt crept into the hard convictions he held about Thomas's guilt, leaving his stomach churning. Had he missed something during the investigation? Had he accused the wrong man?

Charlotte fussed, and Hannah pushed away from the table. She started pacing. "We need to talk to Julie's friends and family. Her neighbors. No one recognized the artist rendering, but the image from the surveillance video is better. Especially with that scar on his neck. Someone may remember Cash and connect him to Julie."

Lieutenant Rodriguez nodded. "Agreed. Meanwhile, the rest of us will put our efforts toward uncovering Cash's real identity as well as locating him. Something may shake loose there."

There were a few more questions and assignments doled out. Then the meeting broke up. Ryker waited until he and Hannah were the only ones left in the room. She reached into the diaper bag for a blanket but couldn't pull it out with Charlotte sleeping on her shoulder.

Ryker retrieved the knitted fabric for her. "We need to talk about Charlotte. Whoever is behind this—whether Cash is acting on his own or he's been hired by Thomas—won't stop. He's also not interested in hurting the baby."

Hannah sighed. "I know." Tears filmed her eyes. "The safest place for her is somewhere far away from me, but I don't have anyone who can watch her."

Ryker's heart broke for her. It was clear she didn't want to be separated from the baby, but they couldn't continue on this way. He'd been forming a plan since before the bombing and now it was time to implement it. "I have a solution that could work."

TEN

"For the hundredth time, I'm fine, Pam." Hannah shook a rattle to amuse Charlotte, who was strapped in her car seat. They were tucked in the back of Ryker's SUV. Beyond the tinted windows, dusk was just beginning to darken the sky into a rich riot of colors.

Hannah breathed out. She needed to relax, otherwise the tension would bleed into her voice and her friend would worry. The doctors had convinced Pam to stay overnight in the hospital after all. "Charlotte and I are staying with Ryker's family for the time being. We'll be safe there."

Pam's sigh of relief was audible over the phone. "Thank goodness. His dad retired from the Marines. Did you know that?"

"He told me. The ranch also has a security system. Plus Ryker called his cousin to help guard the property. Nathan was a Green Beret and his wife, Hayley, works for the Knoxville Police Department. Before that, she was a military police officer." Hannah met Ryker's gaze in the rearview mirror. Her cheeks heated when he winked. "The ranch will be thoroughly fortified."

"It sounds like Ryker has thought of everything. Not that I'm surprised, mind you. He's always been smart. And his parents are lovely people. They'll take good care of you and Charlotte."

Hannah didn't feel entirely comfortable staying with Ryker's family. It blurred the lines of their relationship even more, and with her growing attraction, that didn't seem wise. But her options were limited. The priority was Charlotte's safety. This was the best solution.

She met Ryker's gaze briefly as he glanced in the rearview mirror. Hannah had the sense he'd picked up on the mix of emotions swirling through her. It only deepened her confusion. They'd worked together for months, yet there'd always been a distinct boundary to their relationship. Spending the entire day together—along with the courthouse attack—had shifted something in their relationship. Suddenly, it was like they were in tune to each other in a way that was unique and disconcerting.

Hannah put her focus back on the conversation with her paralegal. "Enough about me. How are you feeling?"

"Oh, I'm fine. I tried to convince the doctors to send me home, but they insisted I stay, and my daughter was so upset I didn't want to make things worse. Something about a concussion at my age. Old. That's what they called me."

Hannah's lips lifted at the indignation in Pam's voice. "I seriously doubt the doctor called you old."

"Well, he didn't use that word specifically, but that's what he was getting at. Meanwhile, he didn't look a day over twelve. I'm not even sure he graduated from a real medical school." She huffed. "I'll be back in the office tomorrow morning. That much I can promise."

"Don't you dare show your face tomorrow. If I see you, I'll have the deputies drag you right back out."

"Not you too!"

"Are you kidding? Your daughter will come up to the courthouse and tear a piece off my backside if I let you step one foot inside the building." That earned Hannah a hearty laugh. Pam's daughter was just as stubborn and feisty as her mom. Hannah switched the phone to her other ear. "Stay home and rest. We'll talk again tomorrow."

"Hold on. Are you going to interview Thomas about the guy who attacked you? The mysterious Cash."

"I've emailed his attorney requesting a meeting. There's no guarantee Jose will allow Thomas to be interviewed, but it's worth a try anyway." Hannah adjusted the blanket around Charlotte and jiggled the rattle again. This time, the baby grabbed it with her own plump fingers. "We need to find Cash as soon as possible. Thomas should be motivated to help us if he's innocent."

Pam snorted. "That man is not innocent. He's behind this whole thing, that much I can guarantee. Judging from the amount of money hidden behind the bookcases at his offices, Thomas was getting money from somewhere. I always believed he had some kind of drug scheme going."

Almost twenty thousand in cash was discovered by the rangers when they conducted a search of Thomas's offices. He shared the space with his wife. Julie had been a dentist. The money was tucked in a hollowed-out textbook on the top shelf in an area accessible to everyone, including patients and staff.

"Thomas claimed he'd never seen that money before and we can't prove it belonged to him. It could've been Julie's. Or even someone on their staff." She leaned her head against the back seat. "Although, I agree with you. The money indicates Thomas was involved in something illegal. And while his involvement is also likely in these attacks against me, he's too smart to contact Cash himself."

Her paralegal hummed in agreement. "He knows we can pull his cell phone records and track his bank accounts. Thomas is under house arrest, so his movements are limited. Even if he got his hands on a burner phone, it's risky. Especially now that Cash has failed twice. If Thomas is behind this, he'd use a go-between."

"Who? Who on earth would get involved in this?"

Pam didn't hesitate for a moment. "His girlfriend. She has a vested interest in keeping him out of prison. Thomas has promised to marry her and love can make you do stupid things."

Ouch. Hannah didn't want to believe that Lorrie Michaels would be foolish enough to involve herself in criminal activity. The young woman was a nurse who came from a loving family. But Pam had a point. Lorrie had gotten involved with Thomas while he was married.

He'd lied and manipulated her once. Chances were, he could do it again.

She mulled over the idea a bit more with Pam and then hung up.

Ryker caught her gaze in the mirror. "I overheard most of the conversation and I think Pam is on to something, but I'd like to question Thomas before we talk to Lorrie."

"Agreed. I should know by tomorrow morning if Jose will allow us to question his client."

She leaned her head against the back of the seat. The trees beyond the tinted window whipped by as the SUV tires ate up the asphalt. Country music flowed from the stereo. Suddenly, Ryker stiffened. His gaze shot to the rearview mirror and then the side-view one. His fingers flew over the buttons on the steering wheel and Eli's name appeared on the built-in screen on the dashboard. Ringing came over the speakers, cutting off the music.

Hannah sat up straight in her seat and turned around to look at the back window before shifting her attention to Ryker. "What is it? What's wrong?"

"We've got a tail. White Chevy pickup truck. Three cars back. There's mud on his license plates."

She spotted the vehicle just as Ryker's colleague Eli answered and promised to send troopers their way.

The driver of the truck wasn't visible because of the distance between the vehicles. Hannah glanced at Charlotte nestled in her car seat. The baby was playing with the rattle, blissfully unaware of the danger they were in. Her chubby cheeks glowed with vitality and her dark curls bounced with the force of her arm movements. Blue eyes locked on Hannah. So crystal clear, with such innocence reflected in their depths.

Hannah forced herself to smile so Charlotte wouldn't pick up on the tension. Once again, her niece was put at risk. The driver of the truck was hanging back for the moment, but what happened if he launched an attack? Were they going to have a high-speed car chase with the baby in the vehicle?

She chewed on her lip and turned back to view the truck. "Could it be a reporter? They've never followed me home before, but the attack at the courthouse headlined the news this evening. It's possible someone wants a photograph or is planning to ambush me hoping to get a soundbite."

"I considered that, but the mud obscuring the license plate is concerning. I don't think a reporter would bother. It makes me think the truck is stolen."

"Cash?" The sour taste of fear filled her mouth. "Guess I didn't stab him hard enough with that screwdriver after all."

"May not be Cash." Ryker's gaze shot to the side-view mirror again as he deftly changed lanes and increased his speed. "I can't see the driver. I don't want to make assumptions."

That sent another spike of terror streaking through Hannah. The only thing worse than being threatened by one hitman was the concept of being hunted by two. Or more. What a horrifying thought. She gripped Charlotte's car seat as if her arms could keep the baby safe.

"Please Lord, watch over us. Guide us to safety. We put our trust in You and know that Your loving wisdom will see us through whatever comes next. Amen."

"Amen." Ryker echoed. His mouth tightened as he glanced in the rearview mirror. "Hold on, Hannah."

She turned back in time to see the truck speeding up. Whoever was driving was about to make a move. Her heart rate spiked as Ryker also increased his speed. The SUV whipped through two lanes of traffic as he shifted without warning toward an exit. Hannah's seat belt locked. Charlotte, jolted by the movement, cried out. She dropped the rattle.

"Shush, shush." Hannah attempted to comfort the baby even as she glanced back at the freeway. The truck had caught their exit and followed. He was picking up speed. Waning sunlight glinted off the windshield, hiding the driver from view. But his intentions couldn't be more clear. He was going to run them off the road.

"Ryker, he's going to hit us!"

ELEVEN

Ryker's pulse jumped as he registered the precarious position they were in. The truck zoomed closer, set on a collision course. Ahead was a sedan with children visible in the back seat. More vehicles were on the frontage road, all of them full of innocent civilians who could be injured in a collision if he lost control of his SUV and slammed into them. Then there was Hannah and Charlotte. Precious cargo.

What to do? If he didn't move, the truck would crash into him. If he did, would the driver hit the sedan with the kids? Neither option was good. Ryker flipped on his flashers and honked his horn with fury, hoping it would encourage the sedan's driver to speed up. Rude, yes. But this wasn't a time to cater to the normal rules of the road. "Move... move... please move."

The sedan in front of him shot ahead as the driver took the hint and pressed on the gas. It safely exited the ramp into the flow of traffic. But the truck was already on them. His bumper kissed theirs. Ryker's head jerked back with the force of the impact. Charlotte's cries increased in intensity. The truck's engine revved as the driver prepared for another hit. Ryker gripped the steering wheel with both hands and made a calculated decision.

"Hold on, Hannah." He twisted the wheel and sent the SUV into the grass. The all-weather tires gripped the dirt with precision. Aiming for a hole in the vehicles on the frontage road, Ryker ignored the way his body bounced in the seat as they reemerged onto the road. Charlotte's cries became full-on screams. His heart broke for the baby. She and Hannah must be terrified, but there was no time to comfort them. His sole mission had to be keeping them safe.

His gaze shot to the truck. The driver had slammed on his brakes and was attempting to maneuver back into position behind them. Ryker didn't want to give him time to catch up. He kept a steady pressure on the gas pedal as the turn onto a country road appeared. That would work. "Hang on once more, Han. This is going to be rough."

Brake lights would alert the driver of the truck to Ryker's intention. He couldn't slow down before taking the turn. A quick glance in the rearview mirror confirmed no one was behind him except for the white truck, which was once again picking up speed. The driver was determined to hit them. Rage threatened to narrow Ryker's vision. Hurting Hannah was bad enough, but putting Charlotte in danger brought things to a whole new level.

He wrangled his emotions back under control with a deep breath and focused on the turn up ahead. A quick prayer for safety whispered through his heart. Three seconds. Two.

Now.

He took his foot off the gas as he turned the wheel, hand over hand, toward the country road. His breath caught. The SUV's tires clipped the edge of the road, threatening to roll them, but then found purchase. They shot into the opposite lane. Ryker quickly maneuvered them back onto the correct side of the street. He glanced in the rearview mirror in time to see the truck whizz past. But the relief was short-lived. Charlotte's screams continued to fill the cab of the vehicle.

He slowed down. "Hannah, are you two okay?"

"Yes. Charlotte's shaken, but we're not hurt."

Her voice was soothing as she spoke to the baby. Moments later, Charlotte's cries lessened to whimpers and then stopped. Ryker glanced at them in his rearview mirror. Hannah was pale, the faint freckles dancing across her nose standing out in stark relief against her skin. She glanced behind them. "We lost him?"

"For the time being." He quickly called Eli and provided his colleague with an update. "I'm taking Charlotte and Hannah directly to my ranch via a back road. Communicate with the troopers that were in route. See if they can find the truck."

"Will do. Call me if you run into more trouble."

Ryker hung up. "We'll be at the ranch in fifteen minutes."

He stayed on high alert while navigating the country roads and sighed with relief when the SUV bounced over the cattle guard at the entrance of Blue Stone Ranch. A camera hung over the gate, more hid in the trees.

Pecan trees lined the paved path and horses grazed in open fields. Several barns sat in the distance. Bluebonnets dotted the grass leading up to the main house. There was no other sign of the white truck, and while it wouldn't take a criminal long to connect the property with Ryker, the advanced security system made it nearly impossible to conduct a surprise attack.

The tension eased from Hannah's shoulders as the gate closed behind their vehicle. She leaned forward to take in the view. "Wow. This place is beautiful. Did you grow up here?"

"From the time I was thirteen. My dad—Jack—is actually my stepfather." His jaw tightened. "My real father died when I was a baby in a car accident. I never knew him. Jack adopted me when I was fifteen, so I'm officially a Montgomery." He pointed out a small cottage tucked in a grove of pecan trees with its own entrance. "That's my place. My cousin, Walker, and his wife will stay there for the next few days while I take a spare bedroom at the main house."

The setup would make it easier to protect Hannah and Charlotte should anything go wrong. Ryker prayed it wouldn't, but he'd take precaution after precaution anyway.

"You live here with your parents?"

The surprise in her voice brought a smile to his face. He slanted a glance in her direction. "I'm a Mama's boy in all the best ways. She doesn't do my laundry or my cooking, but we take care of each other. After my dad died, it was just the two of us for a long time. Then Jack came into the picture. His huge extended family took us into their fold. The Montgomerys can be loud, and everyone is in everyone else's business, but I love them. If anyone in the family needs help, someone is always there."

Hannah sighed. "That sounds wonderful." She leaned back to check on Charlotte. "My dad died when I was in elementary school and I lost my mom shortly after college. Neither of them had extended family, so it was just my brother and I for a long time. Then he met Danielle, and they got married. She's a foster kid, so no family of her own either."

"What about your late husband? Do you have a relationship with his family?"

"I do, but Patrick was never very close to them. His parents had a troubled marriage, and the household wasn't a happy one." She lifted a narrow shoulder. "It's just me, Ben, and Danielle. The three of us support and help each other. And, of course, we have Charlotte. I wouldn't trade them for the world, although I've always longed for a big family with loads of get-togethers and crazy holidays."

Her tone was wistful, and it threatened to shatter Ryker's heart. The burden on her shoulders, the amount of loss she'd suffered... it was painful to think about. The last thing Hannah needed or deserved was a madman hunting her down. Ryker wanted to do more than protect her. He desired to care for her. To lift some of those boulders she carried with such grace onto his own shoulders.

He caught her gaze in the rearview mirror. "If crazy holidays and get-togethers are on your bucket list, then you're in luck. Montgomerys adopt people into the clan. I wouldn't be surprised if you become an honorary member after one day with my mom and dad." His lips lifted in a smile. "You've been warned."

She laughed in reply, exactly as he'd hoped.

The main house came into view. Ryker parked in the circular drive just as the front door opened. His mother, Zoe, hurried down the porch steps on soft-soled shoes. She was dressed comfortably in slacks and a T-shirt, her silvery hair cropped in a pixie cut that framed her delicate features.

Ryker's dad, Jack, followed behind her. The former soldier walked with long strides, a golden Labrador—Oliver—at his side. A holster rode one hip. Lines wore deep grooves in his face, but for a man pushing seventy, he was amazingly healthy. He was also kind. Jack had come into their lives when Ryker was going through some rough teenage years. He'd never been a bad kid, but admittedly, there'd been poor choices. Especially after Alison died.

Bull riding for one.

His mother had desperately tried to talk Ryker out of it. Jack had merely stood by. His disapproval was unspoken but obvious. After a nasty fall in which Ryker suffered a concussion and nearly had his leg crushed, it'd been Jack who walked into the medical tent and with one sentence changed Ryker's entire attitude.

"If you're gonna risk your life, son, make it count for something."

Ryker suspected his stepfather was talking about the armed forces, but he'd taken the advice in a new direction. Law enforcement. Following in the footsteps of the brave detective who'd hunted down Alison's killer and put him in prison where he belonged. Becoming a Texas Ranger was a way to honor his first love. To use his grief for something purposeful.

Ryker exited the vehicle. Zoe came to a stop in front of him. He kissed her cheek before reaching for the passenger-side door. Hannah hopped out of the truck, holding Charlotte. Introductions were made while Ryker hauled the diaper bag over his shoulder.

"Welcome to our little corner of the world." Zoe grinned broadly at Hannah. "It's been a while since we had visitors, so I'm glad to have some new faces."

"A while?" Ryker's brows shot up. "Cousin Mildred and her crew left three days ago." He elbowed Hannah gently. "This house is more like a hotel. You're lucky to find a free bed with all the comings and goings."

She smothered a laugh before focusing on his parents. "Thank you for opening your home. It's very kind."

"Think nothing of it. As my wife said, we love having visitors." Jack tipped his cowboy hat toward Hannah. "Don't worry a lick about anything while on this ranch. As I'm sure Ryker has told you, the property is secure.

We're glad to have you here, ADA Lawson. I have a lot of respect for law enforcement and that includes prosecutors."

"Thank you. And please call me Hannah."

"Just look at this little cutie." Zoe tickled Charlotte's tummy. The baby grinned in response and then tipped toward the older woman. She caught her automatically, holding Charlotte up high, eliciting more giggles, before placing the baby on her hip. Then Zoe hooked her free arm around Hannah's waist. "Come inside. You must be exhausted after such a long day. I've got your room all ready. You and Charlotte can wash up before dinner."

The two women, along with the baby, went inside.

Oliver ambled over to greet Ryker. The dog was getting up there in years, but he was still good at protecting the property. One more layer of protection. Ryker patted Oliver's soft ears before opening the back seat of the SUV and removing Hannah's overnight bag. After the courthouse attack, a female officer had gone to Hannah's house to pack some belongings for her and the baby.

Jack examined the rear of the SUV. "You've got some damage to the bumper, but it's not bad considering how fast y'all were going." His expression darkened. "What monster would try to run a vehicle off the road with a baby inside?"

"Someone who's determined."

Ryker prayed the steps he'd taken would be enough to keep the baby safe. So far, Charlotte hadn't been targeted specifically, but that was always subject to change. The attacks on Hannah were becoming more daring. Rear-ending Ryker's vehicle had been an act of desperation. Less planned than the courthouse bomb threat. Either they were dealing with two different men or Cash was becoming reckless. Whatever the case, this wouldn't stop.

What would come next?

TWELVE

The next morning, Hannah entered the kitchen, Charlotte on her hip. Sunshine spilled across the tile, bathing the room in a warm yellow glow. Zoe stood at the island. Her hair was half-up, held in place by a clip, a newspaper spread out in front of her as she sipped from a coffee mug. The scent of blueberries and sugar hung in the air. Hannah breathed it in, glancing at the pastry resting on the counter. She didn't know what it was, but it smelled divine.

Zoe glanced up. Her expression brightened with a genuine smile that creased the skin around her eyes. "Good morning, girls. How did you sleep?"

"Like logs. Charlotte never stirred, which is unusual these days. She's growing and teething, which can make for some rough nights." Hannah noticed a wooden highchair already set up next to the kitchen table. She gestured to it. "Is that for Charlotte?"

"It is. I had Jack pull it out of storage." Zoe beamed as

she held out her hands for the baby. "It's old, but steady. More than one Montgomery child has used it over the years."

Considerate. Warmth infused Hannah's insides as Charlotte immediately went into Zoe's arms without so much as a whimper. The baby grinned at her newfound friend and reached for her mouth with a plump hand to inspect the older woman's teeth. Over dinner last night, the two had bonded. Hannah had never seen Charlotte take so easily with a new person. Except for Ryker that is. It seemed the handsome ranger and his mother shared a special ability to win over babies with their gentle nature.

Zoe jutted her chin toward some cloth sacks on the counter. "I hope you don't mind, but Jack went to the grocery store this morning and picked up some extra things y'all might need. Diapers. Formula. Some more baby food. We took note of the brands on the items you used last night and bought more of the same."

Hannah's eyes bulged as she shifted through the sacks on the counter. She couldn't believe how much they'd purchased. There was enough to keep Charlotte in clothes, diapers, and food for several weeks. Jack had also bought new toys, along with a few things for Hannah. "It's incredibly generous. Thank you so much. Please let me know how much everything is and I'll happily pay you back."

"Don't you dare try." Zoe cast a stern look toward Hannah as she settled the baby in the highchair and carefully strapped her in. "We want you and Charlotte to feel comfortable here. If there's anything you need, please let us know."

The kindness of Ryker's family was a godsend. After everything that'd happened in the last two days, it was wonderful to be looked after. Last night's dinner had been a welcome relief from the tension. The conversation had centered on family and funny stories. Ryker's cousin, Walker, and his wife, Hayley, were fresh off their honeymoon and shared pictures of their travels to the Grand Canyon.

It'd been the perfect escape. But she couldn't stay in this joyful bubble forever. Somewhere out there, a killer was figuring out his next move. Hannah needed to do everything she could to stop him.

She poured a cup of coffee and took a sip, hoping it would erase the last traces of sleep from her brain. "Where's Ryker?"

"He's in the office." Zoe selected a jar of baby food from the counter. "He's been working since the early-morning hours. I'm sure you'll want to discuss the case with him. Go ahead. I'll feed Charlotte."

"I don't want to put you out."

"Child, nothing brings me more happiness than tending to this sweet little girl." Zoe handed Hannah a plate loaded with the blueberry pastry before making a shooing motion with her hands. "Go on. We'll be fine."

With coffee and breakfast in hand, Hannah planted a kiss on Charlotte's head before strolling across the living room. The office door was open. Comfortable wingback chairs faced an oak desk covered with papers and a laptop. Double dutch doors were open wide, allowing in a light breeze fragrant with wildflowers and dew. Hannah was transfixed by the beautiful view of rolling fields filled with bluebonnets framed by a stunning blue sky.

"Morning."

Ryker's voice came from across the room. Hannah turned to face him and her breath caught. He was planted in a leather chair, feet propped up on the desk, a legal notepad in his hand. His cheeks were sun-kissed, broad shoulders encased in a button-up shirt that brought out the striking green highlights in his hazel eyes. Jeans molded to his powerful thighs.

Hannah's mouth went dry. She took a sip of coffee to buy time to regain her composure. "Hey. Your mom told me you'd be in here. Hope you don't mind."

"Not at all." His lips curved into a smile that made her heart pick up speed. "Where's Charlotte? With my mom?"

"Yep. She snatched her from my arms first thing." Hannah set her pastry down on a nearby table tucked between the two wingback chairs. "I have a feeling I'm not getting her back."

"I warned you. Montgomerys pull people into the fold." His grin widened as he dropped his feet from the corner of the desk to the floor. "Next thing you know, Mom will show up at your house with casseroles and baby clothes. And don't get me started on Jack. He'll have Charlotte riding a horse before she can walk."

Hannah laughed. His assessment wasn't far off.

"Your family is incredible." She turned to admire the view again. "Thank you for bringing us here, Ryker. The ranch is... peaceful. I didn't realize how much it would matter until the house was quiet and dark. I wasn't scared because I knew we were safe."

She felt rather than saw him come up behind her. Then his hand gently cupped her shoulder. "There's no need to thank me. All I want is to keep you and Charlotte safe."

The genuine emotion filling his voice touched something deep inside her. Hannah had known Ryker for a while, but had she ever truly given him a chance as her friend? Not really. That'd been a mistake. Everything Ryker had done since finding out she was in danger was above and beyond his duty as a ranger or acquaintance. He was a good man. Someone she could lean on. And if she was completely honest, she needed the support.

She also needed to be careful. Her emotions were raw. It would be easy for these feelings for Ryker to develop into something deeper. Friendship was one thing, but after all she'd lost—including her husband—the last thing Hannah needed was a broken heart.

She pulled away from his touch under the pretense of looking at the legal pad he'd tossed on the desk. It was covered in his scribbled writing. Focusing on the attack was easier than dealing with this runaway attraction. "Any news about the case?"

"Troopers located the white truck from yesterday's run-in. The crime lab is going over it, but so far, no fingerprints. Same thing with the van Cash used to escape from the courthouse. Both vehicles were stolen in the hours before each attack from nearby grocery stores."

"I doubt they'll find any useful evidence in either vehicle. Cash is smart enough to wear gloves and we already have his face on video, so he isn't worried about being identified. Do we know his real name yet?"

"Nope. Still working on that. Gavin and Claire are interviewing Julie's family and friends. So far, no one recognizes Cash." He gestured to the legal pad. "I've reviewed Julie's case from the beginning, and honestly, I can't see any lead we didn't follow during our initial investigation that would lead to Cash. Or prove Thomas's innocence."

"Jose emailed me this morning. He's agreed to allow Thomas to be interviewed, but has restricted the questions to Cash only. Maybe we can get some additional information that will help."

Ryker's jaw tightened. "Do you intend to be there for the questioning?"

"Absolutely. I need to hear for myself what Thomas has to say." She paused. "I understand the risks of leaving the ranch, but it can't be avoided. I have a job to do. Charlotte will stay here with your family while we're gone. The meeting is set for eleven this morning at the Fulton County Sheriff's Office. I have a feeling Thomas and Jose are trying to appear cooperative."

"More manipulation?"

"Possibly, but I don't care. I'm willing to take any lead we get. The most important thing right now is learning

Cash's identity so we can find him. The sooner we get him off the streets, the better."

Hannah wanted the man locked up in a jail cell. Not just for her own safety, or for Charlotte's, but also for the general population. Cash had called in a bomb threat and created a panic yesterday. He'd put innocent people at risk while trying to run them off the road. Anyone willing to go that far needed to be behind bars.

Ryker was quiet for a long moment. "There's something we need to discuss before we go anywhere."

THIRTEEN

He had to tell her. Transparency was the only way Hannah would truly understand his intentions and his concerns. The attack at the courthouse had shaken Ryker to the core. He'd spent most of the night running it through his mind over and over, reviewing the mistakes he'd made. If Hannah was determined to leave the safety of the ranch, Ryker couldn't stop her. But there needed to be an understanding between them.

He let out a long breath. "When I was fifteen, I started dating a sweet girl in my class. Alison. Her family had recently moved to town, and we hit it off right away. It was puppy love. The kind of summer romance when the most exciting thing that happens is holding hands and a kiss on the cheek."

Hannah's lips curved up slightly, even as her brow crinkled with confusion. She didn't know where he was going with this story, but was kind enough to just listen. It made things easier. Ryker rarely talked about Alison. His family knew, of course, but only one person in his ranger unit did. Eli. They'd grown up together, and Eli had known Alison as well. Both of them had attended her funeral.

"One day, after swimming at the lake, Alison and I were riding our bikes home. She wanted to stop at a local gas station to grab some chocolate and a soda." Ryker remembered the wind blowing against his face as they pedaled down the country lane. Alison had thrown her head back and laughed when she beat him to the gas station. Her dark hair shimmered in the sunlight. Recalling those last happy moments brought a lump to his throat. He swallowed it back down. "We'd only been inside the gas station for a minute when a masked gunman entered."

Hannah inhaled sharply. Her blue eyes locked on his face, and it was too much for him to look at her. Ryker turned and walked to the open balcony doors. Bluebonnets danced in the field. Down by the barn, Jack was leading a horse across the paddock. Walker and Hayley weren't visible. Probably conducting a perimeter check.

Once again, Ryker pulled in a deep breath and forced himself to continue. "I saw him come into the gas station. The gunman. My first instinct was to hide. I pulled Alison down, clapped a hand over her mouth, and whispered for her to stay quiet. Initially she did. We stayed crouched behind a rack of potato chips while the robber demanded cash from the register. He became irate at the amount of money, convinced the clerk was holding out on him, and then..."

Ryker closed his eyes. Heard the echo of the gunshots. "He killed the clerk in cold blood. Alison freaked. She wriggled away from me, jumped up, and started running. I don't think she had any actual plan. Her instincts had taken over. I tried to stop her before—"

The memory of that day slammed into Ryker with the force of a freight train. It stole his breath. Hannah must've sensed the whirlwind of emotion inside him because she came closer. Her hand landed between his shoulder blades. A simple gesture, one of comfort and friendship, that reached inside and ripped open the scabs covering his heart. Tears pricked his eyes. "The gunman shot her. Then me."

A phantom pain in his side burned. "I was fortunate. The bullet only grazed my stomach. I have a scar, but that's minor compared to what could've happened. Alison wasn't so lucky. She died instantly. Only fifteen years old. Murdered while trying to buy a chocolate bar and a soda."

"I'm so sorry. I can't imagine how painful that must've been for you."

The compassion in her voice wasn't surprising, but it touched Ryker all the same. He turned and took her hand in his. Studied the delicate bones, her porcelain skin a contrast to his deeper olive tone. "It was, but I have a reason for sharing this story with you now. In the court-house yesterday, I tried to get you to leave with me, but you took off after Charlotte. It wasn't a mistake—I'm not saying that—but something like that can't happen again. The minute we leave this ranch, your life is in my hands."

Hannah was a strong-willed woman used to calling the shots. In hindsight, Ryker should have stationed a deputy with Pam and Charlotte. A foolish error that'd given Cash an opportunity to abduct Hannah and the baby. But even if he'd taken that precaution, would Hannah have listened to reason? Or left the building without her niece? Probably not.

Ryker lifted his gaze to hers. "There are three things I take seriously: my faith, my family, and my job. As I said yesterday, nothing will prevent me from keeping you safe. But I need your cooperation. In dangerous situations, every second counts. I may ask you to do things you disagree with. You can't argue. Or question me." His tone brooked no argument. "In a crisis, I have the final say. Do you understand?"

She was quiet for a long moment. "You're asking me to trust you implicitly."

"Yes, I am." It was a tall order, especially since they didn't know each other well. Ryker wasn't oblivious to that fact. "It's the only way this will work, Hannah. Anything less puts both our lives at risk."

Silence descended between them. Ryker let it. He knew she was mulling over everything he said. Her gaze drifted over his shoulder to the field beyond the open balcony doors before finally settling back on him. Hannah gently squeezed his hand. "Okay. You have my word that I'll do what you say in a crisis without question."

Relief washed over him as he let out the breath he'd been unconsciously holding. "Thank you."

"No, thank you. For everything. Charlotte and I wouldn't be here today if you hadn't raced back into the courthouse to find us. Then you protected us yesterday from being run off the road." She studied his face with that all-knowing gaze. "But I want to make one thing very clear, Ryker. You aren't responsible if something happens to me. Not everything is within your control. There's no way anyone could've predicted the bomb threat."

"Maybe not, but if anything happens to you, I'll blame myself. It's who I am."

She released his hand and stepped forward before wrapping her slender arms around his waist. Her embrace was unexpected but not unwelcome. Ryker pulled her closer. The scent of her perfume was like a balm on his raw emotions. Her compassion and understanding continued to knock down the walls he'd built to protect himself from romantic entanglements.

Ryker wanted to stop it, but didn't know how. He couldn't push Hannah away any more than he could stop breathing. Nor did he want to. But what kind of future could they have? Was he prepared to truly risk getting hurt if something happened to her? Worse, what if Hannah was killed on his watch?

The thought absolutely terrified him, as did the knowledge that he was treading dangerously close to something he'd successfully avoided since Alison's death.

A broken heart.

FOURTEEN

Three hours later, Hannah stood in the electronics room at the Fulton County Sheriff's Department. A deputy manned the computer station. Multiple screens faced them, one for each interview room. Only one was on. She watched as Thomas and his attorney were led inside by Texas Ranger Eli Goodwin. He politely asked them to wait before backing out and shutting the door.

Beside her, Ryker hooked his thumbs in his pant pockets. Hannah's focus should be on the task ahead of her, but somehow her attention kept being dragged back to the handsome lawman. Their conversation from earlier kept replaying in her mind. So much about Ryker fell into place once she learned about Alison. The haunting look that sometimes came into his eyes, the passion he had for his cases, the flippant way he approached dating, and his need to keep romantic relationships casual.

He'd experienced deep loss. It was something Hannah was very familiar with, and her heart broke for the impact it made on his life. She was also touched he'd shared the story with her. Responsibility for Alison's death wasn't Ryker's burden to carry, but Hannah sensed he wouldn't listen to that argument.

Was it even her place to convince him? Maybe not, but she wasn't the kind to walk away from a friend in pain. If there was some way to help, even a little, she had to try. But first, they needed to find Cash.

The door to the electronics room opened and Eli slipped inside. Hannah had worked several cases with him since joining the District Attorney's Office. He was smart and dedicated. Very serious. The type of law enforcement officer who followed every rule and analyzed the situation from all angles. Hannah secretly thought Eli was the kind of guy she should date, but there were absolutely no sparks between them.

That point was never clearer than right now. Standing next to Ryker, it seemed every cell of her body was tuned to him. It bothered and thrilled her all at the same time.

"Well, I can say right from the get-go that Thomas doesn't seem nervous at all." Eli scowled at the monitor. On screen, Thomas had taken a seat and was nursing a bottle of water while chatting with his attorney about a tennis match he'd played earlier this morning. "If he hired Cash to attack you, he should be concerned about what we might've uncovered since yesterday."

"Not Thomas." Ryker rocked back on his heels. "The guy's a master manipulator and believes he's the smartest person in the room. I think this whole interview is a game."

"Doesn't mean we can't glean some information from it." Hannah collected her notepad and then straightened her shoulders. "Here's the plan. We're going to play good prosecutor, bad cop. I'm going to convince Jose and Thomas that I'm on their side. Namely that I'm seriously thinking about dropping the murder charges given these new developments in the case. Ryker, you need to act ticked off and annoyed that the rangers are being asked to reopen their investigation." She arched her brows, a teasing grin playing on her lips. "Think you pull it off?"

"Not if you keep smiling at me like that." His eyes sparked with humor. "It's distracting."

She caught the teasing note in his voice and appreciated the way he'd played off their argument yesterday at the courthouse. Hannah lightly smacked him with her notepad. "Shut up."

Eli's brow crinkled with confusion as his gaze drifted between the two of them, but he didn't say a word. Still, Hannah's cheeks heated in response as she belatedly realized they'd been flirting. *Flirting*. She and Ryker. That'd never happened before. A sure sign that whatever was transpiring between them was growing by the second.

Then again, maybe not. Ryker was a notorious flirt. Now he was just treating her like every other female in his presence.

Hannah cleared her throat and once again straightened her shoulders. "Let's do this."

Together, they walked down the hall to the interview

room. Jose rose to politely shake their hands. His suit was impeccably tailored, his tie dark blue to match the pinstripes in his shirt. Hannah settled in the chair across from Thomas. His expression grew serious as Ryker read him his rights, but it felt like a carefully placed mask rather than genuine emotion.

Jose adjusted his cufflinks. "For the record, Dr. Anderson has come in for a voluntary interview in order to aid law enforcement in their investigation into the murder of his wife and the attacks on you, ADA Lawson. He maintains his innocence in both matters. We hope his cooperation is noted."

"It is." Hannah nodded. "Thank you, Dr. Anderson, for coming in to speak with us today. As I'm sure your lawyer has explained, the man who attempted to kidnap me from the courthouse bears a striking resemblance to the man you identified as Cash." She placed a still photograph taken from the courthouse surveillance video next to the artist rendering done after Thomas came forward about being threatened by the drug dealer on the table. "As you can imagine, this new development is causing me to question everything we know about Julie's murder."

Thomas glanced at his attorney before looking back at her. "What does that mean? Are you going to drop the charges?"

"I'm seriously considering it." She tossed a hostile look in Ryker's direction. The lawman was slumped in his chair, glowering like he'd been chewed out by the school principal. "The Texas Rangers have requested time to investigate. I've reluctantly given them some leeway."

She turned back to Thomas and let some sympathy leak into her expression. "Of course, any information you can provide about the man who threatened you would be helpful."

He scraped a hand through his hair. "I've been over this story with the police again and again, but I'll do anything to help you find Julie's real killer." Thomas's chin trembled. "All I've ever wanted was justice. For her and my unborn baby."

The words sounded good, but the emotion behind them felt forced. As if Thomas was playacting. Hannah understood why Ryker immediately suspected him of Julie's murder. People grieved in all kinds of ways, but this... it was off. She couldn't pinpoint why though.

Hannah picked up a pen. "Let's start at the beginning. When did the man approach you?"

"It was about two weeks before Julie was murdered. I stayed late to finish charting, and when I walked to my car in the parking lot, he appeared out of the darkness. The way we were positioned, he blocked access to my vehicle. The man identified himself as Cash and said he had a business offer for me. If I wrote prescriptions for painkillers to certain clients, he'd make it worth my while. Of course, I immediately refused. That's when he threatened to hurt someone I love if I didn't comply."

"Did he attempt to harm you?"

"No, just scare me. Cash took off when he heard police sirens coming down the street. I considered reporting the incident, but I was tired and it was late. Law enforcement would have to take my statement, they'd want to search the parking lot, etc. I wanted to get home. The next morning, my office was slammed with patients and..." Thomas shrugged. "I forgot about the whole thing."

Sure. That sounded completely reasonable. Hannah lifted a brow. "Are you often approached in the parking lot by scary men threatening to kill you?"

"No, but we do get people who come into my office looking for pain medication, which I don't prescribe. Narcotics addiction is a problem across the US. While Cash was more aggressive about it than most, I figured he was high when he threatened me. I'd never seen him before, and since he didn't hurt me, let it go. That is until..." He grabbed his water bottle and took a long drink. Tears shimmered in his eyes when his gaze met Hannah's again. "When Julie was killed, I was a wreck. It never occurred to me that the two incidents were linked until weeks later. The moment I thought of it, I called Ranger Montgomery to explain what'd happened."

"There's one thing you forgot to mention when we interviewed you about Cash though." Ryker pointed to the scar creeping across the man's face in the surveillance photograph. It was absent in the artist's rendering. "This scar doesn't look like something you'd forget if you were standing face-to-face with a man."

"Excuse me, Ranger Montgomery." Jose sniffed. "I understand your reputation is on the line here, but surely you aren't attempting to blame my client for your shoddy police work."

Ryker's neck heated and he opened his mouth to respond, but Hannah cut him off with a look. His lips mashed shut, and he promptly leaned back in his chair with just the right amount of attitude. Honestly, the man should get an award for his acting skills.

Hannah turned back to Thomas. "Did you notice the scar during your interaction with Cash in the parking lot?"

He glanced at his lawyer and waited for Jose to nod before answering. "No. The altercation happened at night and I didn't get a good look at his face. Part of it was in the shadows. Plus he was playing with a large hunting knife. I spent most of my time looking at that."

"It's common for victims to pay more attention to the weapon than to the perpetrator's face." Jose smoothed a hand down his tie. "Mr. Anderson didn't purposefully leave out the scar when working with the sketch artist."

Hannah resisted the urge to roll her eyes. The artist sketch was detailed. If Cash had truly been standing in the shadows, then Thomas wouldn't have been able to describe him so well. But challenging them with that fact wouldn't help gain their cooperation.

Instead, she pushed the photograph closer to Thomas. "Other than the altercation in the parking lot, have you ever seen this man before?"

"I've been racking my brain since Jose showed me this picture yesterday. The scar is distinctive. I recalled seeing a patient in our waiting room with a similar mark on his neck. I can't swear the man is the same one that attacked me, but..." Thomas frowned. "It's possible he was one of Julie's patients."

Julie's? This took a turn Hannah wasn't expecting. Her mind whirled. Julie had been a dentist. She and Thomas had shared a waiting room and some staff, but operated separate offices. "When was this?"

"About a month before she was murdered. I only got a glimpse of the guy, so I can't be certain. The person you should talk to is Lorrie Michaels."

Ryker's brows shot up. "Your mistress? Why should we ask her?"

Thomas barely glanced at him. His attention was locked on Hannah, as if willing her to believe him. "For starters, Lorrie and I broke up a while ago. She has no reason to lie for me. And second, you should ask her about Cash because she was working as Julie's office manager during the time frame in question."

"I thought Lorrie worked as your nurse." Hannah studied the man across from her. Thomas was definitely guiding them down a certain path. No matter how innocent and helpful he tried to be, she was more and more convinced of his guilt. Could she prove it in court though? Right now, Jose and Thomas were laying out the argument they'd present to the jury, and Hannah had to admit, it was compelling.

"Normally, Lorrie did work as my nurse, but Julie's office manager had a car accident in January. She was out for weeks. Lorrie filled in since she knew the billing and how that side of the office was run." He tapped on the photograph. "I think this man came in around mid-February, but Lorrie could tell you for certain. She's got excellent recall for patient faces and their medical history. Talk to her."

Hannah's suspicions deepened. The conversation she'd had with Pam yesterday replayed in her mind. Had Thomas and Lorrie teamed up to convince everyone he was innocent of Julie's murder? How did Cash play into everything? And what about the stash of money discovered in the bookcase at the Anderson's offices?

Jose wouldn't allow Thomas to answer any of those questions, so Hannah held them back. "We'll speak to Lorrie."

"Good." Thomas's gaze turned pleading. "I made serious mistakes in my marriage, ADA Lawson. I cheated on my wife. I hurt her emotionally, and I'll have to live with that for the rest of my life. But I didn't kill her." His voice broke on a sob. "I loved her. Find whoever did this. Please."

Hannah clicked her pen closed. "I will." She met his gaze dead-on, conviction bleeding into her voice. "I promise you, Dr. Anderson, I won't stop until whoever is responsible for Julie's murder is behind bars."

FIFTEEN

Ryker watched as Thomas and his attorney left the sheriff's department. His gut was churning and his temper piping hot. Pitching his voice low to keep everyone in the bullpen from overhearing, he turned to Hannah. "Why did you do that? You practically drew a bull's-eye on your chest by challenging Thomas with that promise to go after whoever was responsible for Julie's murder."

"I already have a bull's-eye on my chest, in case you haven't noticed." Her eyes flashed with determination. "I refuse to allow him to bully me. Before today, I had my doubts about his involvement, but now... he's definitely up to something. We need to interview Lorrie, along with the other staff members. I want to know if Cash was actually Julie's patient or if he's lying about that."

"Do you think he's telling the truth about breaking up with Lorrie?"

"I don't know. Maybe. After news about their affair

hit the media, she moved jobs and cities to get away from everything. Lorrie never believed Thomas had killed Julie, but the stress of this situation may have been too much for their relationship."

The door to the electronics room opened. The sheriff, along with Hannah's boss, exited. From the grim looks on their faces, they'd listened to the interview. Claire nodded toward Ryker and Hannah before peeling off toward a cubicle where Gavin was working.

Bruce approached them on long strides. His cheeks were flushed, as if he was ready to explode. "Hannah, could I have a word, please?"

His tone indicated it wasn't a request. Hannah glanced at Ryker briefly before following her boss to a glass-enclosed conference room. Bruce shut the door behind them and immediately started yapping. His expression morphed into something hostile, and his posture towered over Hannah's petite frame. Fresh anger flared as Ryker's hands balled into fists. He took a step forward, but a firm hand grabbed his arm.

"Don't." Eli's voice was low and commanding. "He's the District Attorney. It's not a smart career move to interfere in an argument between him and his subordinate."

Ryker didn't give a fig who he was. He shook off Eli's hand and marched forward. "He's aggressive. Hannah doesn't deserve to be talked to like that. Especially after everything she'd been through these last few days."

"She can hold her own." Eli circled around to block Ryker's path, this time placing a hand squarely in the center of his chest. "Trust me, you go in there and Hannah will tear you apart later. This is her boss. Her job. Let her handle it."

Ryker peered over Eli's shoulder and saw his friend was right. Hannah wasn't yelling at Bruce, but it was clear from her body language that she wasn't backing down either. Bruce started to say something, and she cut him off, punching her finger on the table for emphasis.

Whatever she said caused him to spin away from her and start pacing the room. Hannah kept talking.

Ryker blew out a breath, letting the tension in his shoulders ease. "I'm good. Unless he gets in her face again. Then all bets are off."

Eli dropped his hand. "I never thought I'd see the day. Ryker Montgomery in a twist over a woman." He gave him a knowing look. "Just be careful, man. She's been through a lot. Don't mess with her heart unless you plan on taking it seriously."

"You think I don't know that?"

"I think you've put your heart in a vault since Alison died and kept it there, which has led to some stupid choices in relationships. Fear can cause us to do messed up things. Take it from someone who's been there. There are some decisions and actions you can't take back. Some hurt you can't undo."

Ryker had the sense Eli was talking about his ex-fiancée. They'd broken up five years ago, and he hadn't been the same since. His friend never discussed what'd happened. Clearly whatever it was, it'd had an impact. And Ryker had to admit, Eli had a point. He shouldn't be flirting with Hannah or pursuing her romantically until he got his act together.

"Your advice is noted." Ryker's gaze drifted again toward Hannah. She was still speaking to Bruce, her expression calm but determined. The woman was downright amazing. After everything she'd been through over the last few days, she still fought for what was right. "The last thing I want to do is hurt her. I'll figure it out."

"Let me know if you need a friendly ear." Eli clapped him on the shoulder. "You're a good guy, Ryker, and you deserve happiness. What happened with Alison wasn't your fault. I hope someday you come to realize that too."

Before he could respond, the door to the conference room opened and Bruce stormed out. He marched across the bullpen toward the exit. Hannah lowered herself to a chair and placed her head in her hands. Her shoulders slumped. She looked exhausted and emotionally taxed.

Ryker moved around Eli and made a beeline for the conference room. He shut the blinds so everyone in the bullpen couldn't see them. Then he crossed the room and placed a hand on the back of Hannah's neck. He gently kneaded the tense muscles. "Are you okay?"

She shook her head. "Bruce is frustrated. Someone is leaking details of the case to the media, and they're tearing him apart for not forcing me to drop the charges. It doesn't help that Thomas is his friend. Bruce believes he's innocent and listening to today's interview only reinforced that idea." Hannah dropped her hands. "I convinced Bruce to give me a bit more time, but he's running out of patience."

"He recused himself from this case. Can he force you to drop the charges?"

"Yes. He only recused himself for political reasons. With the media tearing him apart, it's becoming more costly to pursue the case." Her jaw firmed. "I'm sure Thomas is behind the leaks. Or his attorney is. But proving that will be impossible and a waste of time. Thomas's trial starts in five days. His lawyer will claim Cash killed Julie, and right now, I have no way of refuting that."

"We're no closer to identifying him, but there are still avenues to pursue."

"Like Lorrie." She rose from her chair. "Let's go see what she has to say."

SIXTEEN

Lorrie Michaels lived in a high-rise building on the outskirts of Austin. A doorman kept unwanted visitors—like reporters—away, giving her a semblance of privacy. Still, Hannah caught more than one lurking photographer on the street outside the building as they signed in before taking the glass elevator to the penthouse floor. The doors swished open directly into Lorrie's apartment.

She was standing in the entryway, waiting for them, dressed in workout gear. Lorrie was thirty-five, but she could've easily passed for someone a decade younger. Her trim figure and bleach blonde hair gave her the resemblance of a living Barbie doll. It'd been a while since Hannah had seen her, and there were slight changes to Lorrie's face—fuller lips and smoother skin—as if she'd undergone cosmetic procedures.

"ADA Lawson. Ranger Montgomery." Lorrie shook each of their hands and then waved forward. "Come in.

Can I get either of you something to drink? Some water or coffee?"

"I'd love a glass of water, if it's not too much trouble." Hannah's gaze swept across the spacious living room as they moved deeper into the apartment. It was decorated in a mix of ivory, cream, and silver. Large windows provided sweeping views of the city. The throw on the couch was designer and the artwork on the walls appeared original. The floor plan was an open-concept so the living space flowed into a kitchen with marble countertops and state-of-the-art appliances.

This was a definite upgrade from the tiny home Lorrie had when she was living in Fulton County. Either she'd come into a great deal of money recently, or she'd been living frugally before. From the faint purse of Ryker's lips, he was thinking exactly the same thing.

"Your home is beautiful." Hannah raised her voice so it could carry across the distance to the kitchen, where Lorrie was preparing glasses of ice water on a silver tray. "Are you still working at the children's hospital?"

"No. I took a job as a traveling nurse."

"Traveling nurse?" Ryker asked, taking a seat next to Hannah on the couch.

"When a hospital is short staffed, they hire agencies to fill those positions temporarily. The job requires me to travel to different cities for months at a time, but the pay can be three or four times a normal nurse's salary." She carried the tray into the living room. "It's the only way I could afford an apartment like this."

Hannah made a mental note to review Lorrie's financial records. It was possible she was telling them the truth, but given the price tag associated with some of the items in the apartment, she'd need more than a traveling nurse's salary to explain their presence.

She accepted the glass of water from Lorrie with a smile. "How often do you travel?"

"Oh lots. After…" Lorrie's gaze skittered away from Hannah's toward the windows overlooking the city. "Well, I needed a distraction and dove into work. In fact, you're lucky to have caught me. I just finished a contract yesterday with a hospital in San Diego. They wanted me to stay longer, but it was impossible since I've been subpoenaed to testify at Thomas's trial next week." She licked her glossy lips. "Is that why you're here? To discuss the trial?"

"Not exactly." Hannah set her glass on a coaster. "Have you been watching the news?"

"Heavens no. Those nasty reporters tore my life apart and practically sent me into a depression with everything that was said after Julie died. I don't watch the news or use social media. Too much vitriol." Her gaze skipped between Hannah and Ryker. Her muscles stiffened. "Why? Has something happened to Thomas? We broke up months ago and I haven't talked to him since, but I noticed there were reporters downstairs this morning when I went to the gym."

"Thomas is fine." Hannah opened her leather file folder and removed the still image of Cash taken from the surveillance video at the courthouse. She handed it to Lorrie. "Do you recognize this man?"

The other woman frowned, although her mouth didn't turn down very far. "That looks like a former patient of Julie's. I recognize him because of that scar on his neck."

Hannah kept her gaze locked on Lorrie. "Do you know his name?"

"Um... let me think. He only came in a time or two while I was working as Lorrie's office manager. Cathy had a horrible car accident and was out for months..." She squinted at the photograph. "He had a problem with a tooth in the upper right quadrant. Goodness, what was his name?"

Lorrie seemed genuinely perplexed, but Hannah silently reminded herself that Thomas's ex might simply be an excellent actress. It was hard to get a bead on the other woman. Her lack of facial expression, probably due to Botox, made it difficult to deduce whether she was lying.

"Edward..." Lorrie shook her head, her blond hair shimmering in the late afternoon sunlight. "No, Dusty." Her lips curved into a wide smile and her eyes brightened with triumph. "Dusty Stillman."

Hannah glanced at Ryker as he rose from the couch with his cell phone already in one hand. He moved away from them toward the far end of the living room before lifting the device to his ear, probably to run Dusty's criminal record. She let out the breath she'd been holding. "Are you sure?"

"Positive. He came in twice, both times in late February." Her brow crinkled slightly. "Why are you asking?"

Hannah ignored her question. "What were Dusty's interactions with Julie like?"

Lorrie lifted a slender shoulder. "I'm not sure. I only handled the front desk."

"Did Dusty ever ask about Dr. Anderson?"

"Thomas? No." Her gaze narrowed. "What is going on?"

"We believe this man is behind the attack on Thomas in the parking lot a few weeks before Julie was murdered."

Lorrie shot off the couch. "You mean he was telling the truth about that?" Her chin trembled as tears filmed her eyes. "How... Why..." She shook her head, her blond hair swaying. "I accused him of lying, said horrible things to him when we broke up."

Her voice came out on a sob. Hannah rose and grabbed a few tissues from a nearby table before returning to Julie's side. "We don't know anything definitive yet. The investigation is still in its early stages."

"But could Thomas really be innocent of Julie's murder?"

"You doubted his innocence?" Hannah kept the shock vibrating through her from bleeding into her voice, but it took effort. Lorrie had been Thomas's fiercest defender throughout the course of the investigation.

"I..." Lorrie sank back to the couch. "No. I don't

know. Thomas is very good at painting a picture of what he wants you to see. I'm not sure anyone really knows who he is or what he's capable of."

Hannah settled into the seat next to her. "Is that why you broke up?"

She nodded and swiped at the tears on her face. "I was foolish to get involved with a married man. My parents raised me better than that, but when Thomas hit on me, I was at a low point. I'd broken up with an abusive ex and was desperate for attention and love. Thomas swore his marriage to Julie was over. They slept in separate bedrooms and barely talked. He was going to file for divorce, but things took time."

Classic. Hannah had heard this type of story over and over again. Julie was complicit in the affair, but it wasn't unusual for a vulnerable woman to be taken advantage of by a manipulative man. "How were his interactions with Julie at the office?"

"Strained. That's part of the reason I believed him." She let out a long sigh. "They genuinely seemed to have marital trouble. And maybe they were... I don't know. There were a lot of weird things going on at the office in the months before Julie was killed."

"What things?"

"Billing issues. Staffing problems. Several people were fired from Julie's side of the practice and replaced by temps. It was chaotic. Julie was incredibly tense in a way I'd never seen her before. Once I forgot to log out of the main computer before leaving the office and she flipped out. At the time, I thought the issues with Thomas were making her tense, but in the last several months since we've broken up, I've reconsidered." She chewed her lip. "Julie was worried about something and becoming paranoid."

"Paranoid? Can you give me a specific example of an incident that made you think that?"

"Well, there was the computer incident. That was weird because it wasn't the first time I'd done that. Then I walked into an exam room one time and she nearly jumped out of her skin. In March, she suddenly decided not to see any new patients. Once someone popped in with an emergency issue and Julie adamantly refused to see him. I had to talk her into it because I could tell the patient was in a great deal of pain."

"Refusing to see an emergency walk-in was strange behavior?"

"Very. Julie was patient-oriented and never turned away anyone who needed her. More than once, she stayed late to handle a patient having an unexpected tooth issue." Lorrie twisted the tissues between her hands. "It's hard to explain. The way Julie reacted when I asked her to see the patient... it was out of character. The only way I can describe it is paranoid."

"Did she think the man would harm her?"

"I didn't get that sense. More like suspicion. As if he was lying about his problem. It was so strange. Like I said, at the time, I thought she was just having issues with Thomas. After her murder, he and I were talking, and I told him about these incidents. He convinced me not to tell the police. Thomas was worried that Julie's strange behavior would make him appear more guilty. By that time, I was in love with him, so I kept quiet."

"And you didn't think to tell the police after you two broke up?"

"I did, but so much time had passed.... I wasn't sure it was important. Thomas is a liar, but I'm not convinced he killed Julie. Deep down, I think he truly loved her." She picked up the photograph of Cash from the coffee table. "If this is the man who attacked him in the parking lot, doesn't that mean he was telling the truth about what happened? Maybe Julie was involved with these people somehow."

It was something to consider. Maybe Thomas was telling the truth about the incident in the parking lot, but wasn't honest about his conversation with Cash. A half-lie. It was also possible Lorrie was lying now. It seemed very convenient that she spilled all this information a few days before Thomas's trial.

Hannah studied the other woman. "What caused you and Thomas to break up?"

"It wasn't one single thing. I discovered he was lying to me. Had been the entire time we were together. First, I learned he never attempted to file for divorce. Then it came out that Julie was pregnant at the time of her death, which meant he lied about the state of their relationship. Thomas convinced me things weren't how they seemed in the media. I stupidly believed him. But over time, more and more lies piled up. Plus the reporters were hounding me every day. It all became too much to handle."

New tears filled her eyes. "We had a huge fight. I said some awful things to him. Accused him of lying about the incident in the parking lot just like he did about everything else. I stormed out of his house and haven't seen him since."

"He hasn't attempted to contact you?"

"No, he tried. Sent flowers. Called. I refused to talk to him." Her shoulders sagged. "I can't do this with him anymore. I want to get this trial over with and move on with my life."

Ryker hung up his cell phone and rejoined them. "I'm sorry, Ms. Michaels, but we need to go. Thank you for your time."

His tone was curt and abrupt, but he gently reached down to take Hannah's arm and pulled her into a standing position. She wriggled away long enough to grab her leather file folder, say goodbye to Lorrie, and then hurried to catch up with him at the elevator.

He was already inside, holding the door open for her with one strong hand. The second she slipped past him, Ryker stepped back and the doors swished closed.

She turned to face him. "What are you doing? I wasn't done—"

"It's Kristin."

The look on his face stole her breath. She instinctively took one step backward, as if to ward off what Ryker was about to tell her. It wasn't good. Bile churned in her stomach. She'd had her problems with Kristin, but would never wish any ill will on her ambitious colleague.

Hannah's back bumped into the far wall of the elevator. "What about her?"

Ryker reached for her, his palms cupping her biceps as if he was afraid her knees would give out with the next bit of information. Warmth and sympathy tangled in his hazel eyes. "I'm sorry, Han. She's been murdered."

SEVENTEEN

The crime scene was organized chaos. Deputies were stationed at the perimeter to keep neighbors and the media back. Red and blue lights strobed, cutting through the night. A coroner's van was tucked between a marked patrol car and a crime scene unit vehicle. Several deputies were walking down the street. One strolled up a neighbor's driveway to knock on the front door.

They were canvassing. Deputies would talk to the neighbors, ask to look in the backyard, and request video footage from any surveillance on the home in the hopes it would help identify the killer. Ryker prayed something would come of it, but he wasn't holding out much hope. Cash... no, Dusty Stillman, had planned every attack carefully.

His rap sheet wasn't long, but the crimes were serious. Armed robbery, drug dealing, and murder. He was a professional criminal who'd evaded significant prison time by intimidating witnesses or plea bargaining down to a less serious charge.

Ryker pulled his SUV next to the curb but didn't kill the engine. "You don't need to do this, Hannah. Claire and Gavin are on scene. They can call us later."

"No." She reached for her door handle. "Kristin was my mentee. She worked for me and that makes her my responsibility. I'm doing this."

Her tone brooked no argument. Stubborn woman. She was ghost pale and had barely uttered a word the entire car ride back to Fulton County, but nothing would stop her from standing up for Kristin. For doing what she could to catch the younger lawyer's killer. It was admirable, but not surprising. Still, Ryker feared she wasn't emotionally prepared to handle what lay inside the small two-bedroom house.

He placed a hand on Hannah's back as they climbed the driveway. Her muscles were rigid, her expression a professional mask of indifference, but she leaned into his touch slightly. Just enough to let Ryker know she appreciated the support.

Gavin met them in the entryway. His expression was grim. Dark circles shadowed the skin under his eyes and his clothes were wrinkled. He'd put in long hours since the initial attack on Hannah and the bomb threat at the courthouse had only made things worse. The entire ranger team—along with Claire and her deputies—were working overtime to sort through evidence, interview witnesses, and track down leads. Everyone wanted Dusty caught as soon as possible.

Ryker greeted his colleague with a nod. "What can you tell us?"

"Victim has been identified as Kristin Michaels. The body was discovered about two hours ago by her cousin." Gavin removed a notepad from his rear pocket and began reading from it. "Kristin and her cousin were supposed to have dinner tonight, and when she didn't show or answer her cell, the cousin became concerned. She has a key to the house, used it to enter, and discovered Kristin in the bedroom."

A rattling came from the hallway, and a moment later, two coroner's assistants appeared. They navigated a wheeled stretcher with a body bag on top. Kristin. Ryker had been to hundreds of crime scenes, but they never got easier. He didn't want them to. His insides churned as the men wheeled the stretcher out the front door.

Beside him, Hannah's complexion paled even more. Once again, Ryker placed a hand on the small of her back. He wanted to gather her in his arms and carry her out of the house, but that wasn't an option. For starters, it would be unprofessional. And second, Hannah wouldn't want him to. For better or worse, she was determined to see this through. He couldn't stop her, but he could support her.

Hannah swallowed hard and gestured toward the security system. "Was that armed when the cousin entered?"

"No. We conducted a search and discovered a window in the living room had been broken. It seems the killer entered that way. It doesn't appear she ever knew he was in the house. Not until it was too late."

"A broken window and a disarmed security system." Hannah's jaw tightened. "That's just like when I was attacked. I want to see where the attack happened."

Gavin gestured for them to follow him down the short hallway. The primary bedroom was decorated with dark grays and deep purples. A pile of laundry rested in a chair in the corner. Shoes were tossed haphazardly near the dresser. A photograph of Kristin and an older couple rested on the vanity, along with piles of makeup. Her parents? It certainly looked that way. Ryker's heart sank to think of them receiving the news that their daughter had been murdered. He said a prayer for them. That, along with capturing Kristin's killer, was all he could do.

Claire rose from the crouched position she'd been in next to the four-poster bed. Like her husband, her uniform was wrinkled and dark circles shadowed the skin under her eyes. Her hair was pulled into a ponytail, but the blonde strands looked greasy, as if she hadn't had time to wash her hair. His mouth hardened. "The killer screwed up. He cut himself on the glass near the window and left a fingerprint behind." Claire lifted her cell. "The lab just called me. We've got a positive ID. It's Dusty Stillman."

The sheets and comforter had been tangled and dropped to the floor. Blood coated them, along with the carpet. Hannah stared at it before lifting her gaze to the sheriff. "Kristin was stabbed?"

Claire nodded. "Several times and then her throat

was cut. It appears the killer caught her as she was getting ready to go out. A blitz-style attack."

"Just like with me. And Julie." Hannah's voice was hollow. Her jaw tightened. "Did he leave a note?"

Claire shared a look with Gavin. Ryker immediately picked up on their tension. Whatever was in the note was bad. He stepped forward. "Hannah—"

"Don't, Ryker." She gave Claire a steely look, one normally reserved for difficult witnesses in the courtroom. "I want to see the note."

Claire breathed out a long sigh and reached for an evidence bag resting along with a few others on the nightstand. She handed it to Hannah without a word. Ryker's gaze took in the plain white paper, which could've been bought from any office supply store in the county. Shock and horror vibrated through him as he focused on the letter's contents. It wasn't addressed to anyone, but the message was clearly meant for Hannah.

You should have gotten in the van.

Rage unlike anything Ryker had ever experienced swept over him like a tidal wave. It heated his blood. He wouldn't stop until Dusty was in prison for the rest of his life. It didn't matter how long it took or how far Ryker had to go. He would hunt him down and make him pay.

"I..." Hannah swayed, and the note dropped from her fingertips. All the blood had drained from her face.

She bolted from the room.

Ryker ran after her. The night air embraced him as he flew out of the front door. Hannah was standing near his vehicle, bent over, vomiting on the sidewalk in the shadows. He raced to her side and held back her hair until she was done. Helplessness mingled with the rage. It tangled inside him, creating a war that he couldn't sort through. All he knew was that he'd do what it took to protect Hannah. Physically and emotionally.

She straightened, wiping her mouth with the back of her hand. Tears streaked her cheeks. They punched right through Ryker. He opened the door to his SUV and fished some tissues from the center console. He handed them to her. "Here."

She mopped her face while he fetched a bottle of water from an emergency supply in the trunk. Ryker steered her deeper into the shadows to prevent any of the deputies from observing the moment. Hannah was still frighteningly pale. He gently brushed a damp strand of hair off her forehead. She'd been through the wringer the last few days and that note might've pushed her right over the edge. Emotional stress could cause physical symptoms. "I'm going to have an EMT look at you."

"No." She grabbed his hand, stopping him. "I'm okay." Her chin trembled as her voice grew softer. "Don't leave me."

"Never."

The word was out before Ryker could even ponder its implications. He gathered Hannah into his arms. She melted against him, her shoulders trembling as she swallowed down fresh sobs. Ryker just held her. Let her lean on him for as long as she needed. Hannah was one of the strongest women he'd ever met, but everyone had a breaking point.

God, help me comfort her. Give me the right words to say.

Finally, when his shirt was wet with her tears, she pulled back and drained the water. She crushed the bottle in her hand.

He gently took it from her. "This isn't your fault, Hannah. He's trying to get into your head, to make you feel responsible for Kristin's death. But you're not." He placed a finger under her chin until she was forced to look into his eyes. "None of this is your fault. Got it?"

She breathed out and then nodded. "I know. I just... that note was a shock. Sorry for falling apart on you."

"You have nothing to apologize for." He pulled her closer and kissed the top of her head. "Fall apart whenever you need to. I've got you."

She squeezed his waist. "Can you take me back to the ranch? I need to see Charlotte."

"Of course."

Ryker escorted her to the passenger side of his SUV and opened the door before helping her inside. Hannah sagged against the seat and closed her eyes. She had to be exhausted. He was too. The ranger team would continue to work in shifts throughout the night. Hopefully, by morning, Dusty would be in custody.

Headlights shimmered in the rearview mirror for most of the drive home. When Ryker turned on the two-lane county road leading to his ranch, he kept a sharp eye out for any trouble. Man or animal. Deer were frequently crossing the road, especially at night, and had caused more than one accident.

In the passenger seat, Hannah was quiet. She hadn't said a word for the entire ride, lost in her own thoughts. Ryker had the sense she was working through the case rather than beating herself up for not protecting Kristin, so he let her be. Later, Hannah could fill him in on her conversation with Lorrie.

He was struggling with his own theories. Had he missed some vital piece of evidence in Julie's murder? Was Dusty responsible for killing her as well as Kristin? It was possible. Right now, everything he knew about the case should be re-examined.

They passed a dirt road, and a vehicle rumbled out. Suddenly, light blazed off the rearview mirror, blinding Ryker. His heart rate jumped as he realized someone had been lying in wait for them. A roar broke through the night as the oversized truck behind them sped up.

It was on a collision course.

He gripped the steering wheel as his heart rate jumped. "Hold on, Hannah!"

EIGHTEEN

The impact jolted Hannah against the seat. Her belt locked, holding her in place, as her breath stalled. She gripped the door handle. Fear formed a sour taste in her mouth and silent prayers flooded her heart. Dusty had been lying in wait for them. He was determined to kill Hannah and didn't care how it was accomplished or who he hurt in the process.

Ryker swerved to make them a harder target to hit. Another roar came from the truck behind them. Hannah's gaze shot to the side-view mirror. The truck had a large metal grill covering the front bumper and giant tires. Their SUV was powerful, but it was no match for Dusty's vehicle. She scrambled to retrieve her cell phone from the cup holder.

Help. They needed help.

Metal crunched against metal as Dusty rammed them again. Hannah's body listed to the left unexpectedly and her head hit the window. Pain erupted along her temple. Ryker uncharacteristically swore under his breath as he white-knuckled the steering wheel. Their speed climbed as he tried to put some distance between them and Dusty.

Ignoring the ache arching through her scalp, Hannah unlocked her phone. Explaining their situation to a 911 dispatcher would take too long. She chose Eli's name from her contacts and put the call on speaker. He answered on the first ring.

"We're being chased." Hannah spit out details in rapid succession, including their location. "Large truck. Silver or gray. It has a grill on the front bumper and over-sized tires."

"Deputies are in route." Eli's voice was clipped, and it sounded like he was running. "So am I. License plate?"

Hannah glanced in the side-view mirror, but the truck's bright headlights prevented her from getting a clear view. Ryker swerved again, jostling her in the seat. She gripped her cell phone. "It's not visible."

Another roar punctuated her words. Hannah's heart stuttered as the road ahead of them leaned into a sharp curve. Her gaze shot to Ryker. His attention was locked on the street, determination etching grooves across his handsome face, and Hannah knew he'd do everything in his power to get them out of this situation. But would it be enough?

Terror struck her more violently than the vehicles colliding. In an instant, everything became crystal clear. Despite her best efforts not to, she was developing feelings for Ryker. Deep ones. Powerful ones. And protecting her had put his life in danger. Hannah had already lost so many people she cared about. Her parents. Her husband. Her brother was in a war zone and her colleague had just been murdered. She didn't think her heart could take much more.

The truck slammed into the rear of their vehicle. Hannah screamed as the SUV went into a spin. Her cell phone flew from her hand as metal against metal screeched. Glass shattered. Momentum pushed them toward a small drop-off. Trees loomed large, and then the world became topsy-turvy as the SUV rolled over and over.

Hannah's body was shoved by uncontrollable forces like a rag doll. Pain erupted along her shoulder and collarbone as the seat belt once again gripped her. The roar in her ears drowned out everything else.

Suddenly, the vehicle came to a shuddering stop. The scent of pine and earth assaulted her senses. Hannah peeled her eyes open and realized they'd landed upside down on a tree. Branches reached inside her broken window like arms. Pine needles mixed with blood on her clothes. She drew in a shuddering breath and took three seconds to assess her body. Nothing seemed broken. She was alive, and mostly, unharmed.

"Ryker." She twisted her head, ignoring the pain shooting up her neck from a bad case of whiplash. Her pulse shot into the stratosphere again. The side of Ryker's head was covered in blood. It dripped from the thick strands of his black hair onto the roof of the upside-down

SUV. His eyes were closed. Hannah shook his shoulder. "Ryker."

No response.

Tears pricked her eyes as panic threatened to take hold. She wrestled it back. Fumbling with her seat belt, Hannah attempted to release the catch, but hanging upside down prevented the mechanism from disengaging. She pushed against the dented roof as leverage with one hand. Glass bit into the tender flesh of her palm.

"Come on." Her fingers trembled as she shoved at the button to release her seat belt.

Finally there was a click. Hannah landed in a tangled heap onto the broken branches and damaged roof. Quakes trembled through her body as she maneuvered over to Ryker. She held her breath and pressed two fingers against the inner portion of his wrist, searching for a heartbeat.

He was alive.

The relief was so heady, she was dizzy with it. Hannah blinked to clear her vision. She searched for her cell phone among the wreckage, but there was no sign of it. Should she move Ryker? Or leave him be until paramedics arrived? Help was on the way. Eli had been on the phone with them when the accident happened, so he'd send deputies and other first responders.

But how far away were they? Ryker's pulse was strong, but his head wound was bleeding steadily. There was no way to know if he had any other injuries since he was unconscious. Helplessness increased her trembles. She didn't even have anything to stop the bleeding.

A branch cracked.

Hannah froze. She strained to hear over the sound of her ragged breathing and rapid heartbeat. Another rustle reached her ears. Someone was approaching their SUV.

Dusty? It had to be. He was coming to finish the job.

Terror streaked through her. She battled it back and forced her mind to sort through the options. Hannah could slip out of the window and escape, but that would leave Ryker alone and unconscious in the car. He wasn't the target, but there was no way to guarantee Dusty wouldn't kill him. The risk was too great. She couldn't leave.

That only left one choice. Defend.

Hannah reached for the holster strapped to Ryker's waist. She unsnapped the button holding his weapon in place and the gun slid into her hand. The metal felt cold against her heated skin. A Glock 22. She was familiar with this model, had shot it before at a range with her brother. Ben had insisted she knew how to handle a gun, even though she didn't own one. Hannah adjusted her hold on the weapon, slipping her finger next to the trigger.

Another branch cracked. He was close. Coming at them from the right.

Hannah positioned her body to shield Ryker. Her vision narrowed as adrenaline coursed through her veins. Inside her mind, her brother's voice cut through her fear.

Aim the weapon, hold your breath, and squeeze the trigger.

Ben made sure she practiced at the range every

month when he was in town. But Hannah had only shot paper targets, never at a person. Could she actually do this? She sucked in a deep breath to slow her racing heartbeat. Then another. Her trembles slowed and then stopped. There was no choice. Ryker needed her. There was no doubt in Hannah's mind that Dusty would kill them both the moment he reached the SUV.

Another rustle reached her ears. He was almost there.

Please, God. Please protect us. We need You now more than ever.

NINETEEN

Ryker awoke with a jolt.

He groaned. His head was pounding in time with his heartbeat, pain cruising along his scalp from the stitches hidden in his hairline. Sunlight streamed through the curtains, creating a pattern on the carpet. He winced at the brightness and blinked to rid his mind of the last vestiges of his nightmare. It didn't fade quickly. Something about Dusty hurting Hannah. While the sequence of the dream wasn't clear, the terror had been all too real. Ryker's heart rate was through the roof. He sucked in a breath through his teeth to combat the adrenaline coursing through his veins. Then another.

His legs were tangled in the bedsheets and sweat coated his back. Ryker tossed the covers aside. A quick glance at the clock confirmed it was nearly noon. They'd come home from the hospital in the early-morning hours. Doctors had diagnosed him with a concussion and put ten stitches in his scalp. He'd been ordered to rest. Fat chance of that happening.

Not while Dusty was still at large.

The criminal had run them off the road and then approached the battered SUV to finish the job. Hannah, brave woman that she was, readied herself to shoot him if need be. Approaching sirens scared Dusty away before he could get close enough to harm her. He escaped from the scene. Deputies discovered the truck he'd stolen three hours later in an abandoned feed store parking lot. It'd been hauled to the forensic shed for processing, but Ryker wasn't holding his breath. So far none of their efforts had yielded much in the way of results. None of Dusty's family or friends or known criminal associates had seen him in weeks.

Ryker hauled himself to the bathroom. Cuts and bruises covered his body, and every muscle hurt, but he was thankful to be alive. More grateful that Hannah walked away from the accident with nothing more than a few minor nicks from the broken glass. Losing her... worse, being responsible for her injury or death...it jabbed at every one of his insecurities and deepest fears. He hadn't protected Alison during the gas station robbery.

He couldn't fail again. Not with Hannah.

A shower and fresh clothes went a long way to making him feel normal. Ryker left his bedroom and hurried down the hall. The murmur of Hannah's voice filtered from the living room. He rounded the corner to find her on the floor with Charlotte.

The baby was propped into a seated position, her back and side supported by some kind of funny-looking pillow. She whacked at a toy with both chubby hands. Music spilled from light-up buttons. Charlotte squealed with joy. Her happiness made Hannah laugh too. The sound reached right inside Ryker and wrapped around his heart, squeezing it tight. Good heavens, the woman was stunning. Her shiny hair was piled into a messy bun, her face makeup free. Yoga pants and a long T-shirt molded to her slender form. Her feet were bare.

Hannah must've sensed his presence because she glanced up. Her smile widened. "Hey there. How are you feeling?"

"Better now that I see you two." He joined them on the floor. The sounds of rattling pots and pans filtered into the room from the kitchen. "Is my mom cooking lunch?"

"Yep. Eli called a while ago. He's coming here, along with Gavin and Claire, to discuss the case. Your mom is whipping up something for them to eat, and since I haven't spent much time with this little munchkin"—she tickled Charlotte under the chin—"we came in here to play."

"Nice." He enjoyed seeing Hannah happy and relaxed. Especially after yesterday. Ryker patted his pocket and realized he'd left his phone charging in the kitchen last night. "What time are they coming?"

"In an hour." Hannah's gaze assessed him, those gorgeous blue eyes squinting slightly as her attention was drawn to his hair and the wound hidden inside. "You have some more time to lie down, if you want. I was gonna wake you in thirty minutes."

"No, it's okay."

A strand of hair had wriggled loose from her bun. Ryker brushed it away from her cheek to tuck it behind her ear. Hannah's skin was soft. Her breath hitched as his thumb caressed the delicate curve of her chin. A faint scratch marred her porcelain complexion. It was a stark reminder of how close Ryker had come to losing her last night. "How are you doing?"

She reached up to take his hand. "I'm better this morning. I didn't sleep a wink until Eli called from the hospital and told me you'd be okay." Tears shimmered in her eyes. "I was really worried about you. Don't scare me like that again, Ryker. My heart can't handle it."

"Hannah..." A lump formed in his throat. Had any woman ever looked at him like that? With such feeling? Warning bells clanged in his head as Ryker's gaze drifted to her lips. He wanted to kiss her. So much. Sheer willpower held him back. He would never, ever do anything to hurt her. "I want to promise that I'll never put myself in a dangerous situation again, but that's not possible. It's kinda in the job description."

She chuckled. "Yeah. One minor detail." Hannah met his gaze again. "I don't like that you're in danger because of me."

"I'm not in danger because of you. None of this is your fault." He squeezed her hand gently. "And from what Eli said, I'm fortunate to have you on my team. You were ready to risk your life to protect me. Do you know how brave you are? It's incredible. You're incredible."

She blushed. Then her lips curved into a smile. "Keep talking, ranger. I don't get compliments that often."

"A shame. A woman like you should receive compliments every day."

"You think so?" She tilted her head, and then her gaze skittered away from his. "I'm surprised to hear you say it. You've flirted with practically every female in my office. Except for me."

There was a tinge of hurt in her voice. Ryker couldn't let that stand. He trailed a thumb across her knuckles. "Did you ever think that maybe I couldn't flirt with you? It's embarrassing to admit, but you make me nervous."

"Nervous? Why?"

"Because I care about you, Hannah. More than I should." Ryker hesitated but realized he'd waded into deep waters without meaning to. Adding this kind of pressure to an already fraught situation was a bad idea. Hannah had a killer coming for her. The last thing she needed was to be burdened by his emotional problems. He gently pulled his hand away from hers under the guise of twisting a knob on Charlotte's toy. "Forget it. Let's talk about something else."

"I don't want to talk about something else. I'm tired of ignoring what's happening between us." She touched his sleeve. "I care about you too, Ryker. And I'm scared. I've lost a lot of people in my life, and my heart has been pretty battered and bruised. Maybe I'm wrong, but I get the sense you're scared too. The way you treat romantic relationships never made sense until you told me about Alison. Then I realized you've built a wall around that wonderful heart of yours."

Ryker wasn't surprised by Hannah's observations. She was smart and intuitive. His gaze shot to her beautiful face. The compassion and understanding written on her features nearly undid him. "I didn't save her. My screwup cost Alison her life."

"No, Ryker. What happened wasn't your fault, just like what happened with Kristin wasn't mine. The gunman that entered that gas station and killed Alison is the only one responsible."

He opened his mouth to argue but then snapped it close. The situations weren't exactly the same, but... Hannah had a point. The brilliant woman had painted him into a corner. His gaze narrowed. "Excellent move, counselor. You're using my own argument against me."

"I sure am." Hannah leaned closer. "You and I are more alike than either of us realized. Both of us longing to fall in love, but neither willing to take the leap because we're both scared out of our minds."

"So where does that leave us?"

"I'm not sure, but I think we should find out."

Ryker's breath hitched as her gaze dropped to his mouth. Like a magnet pulled of its own volition, he couldn't resist leaning toward her. Hannah needed no encouragement. She met him halfway, and the moment their lips touched, nothing else mattered. Every fiber of his being was focused solely on her. The soft feel of her mouth, the warmth of her skin as he cupped her face to deepen the kiss, and the way she met his passion with her own. He was lost in her. A drowning man who never wanted to resurface.

Where would this end? Ryker didn't know. Both of them could walk away with a broken heart when it was all said and done. Fear was an insidious thing. It crept in at unexpected times and he'd always moved back to a safe position with romantic relationships. He'd never leaned forward.

Hannah made him want to choose differently.

But could he?

TWENTY

Two hours later, Hannah leaned back in her chair with a sigh of contentment. The center of the table was littered with the remnants of lunch. Fried chicken, creamy mashed potatoes, and all the homemade rolls had disappeared. A few lone vegetables littered one platter. The only thing better than the food had been the conversation. Seated around the table were Ryker's colleagues and his family. As if by unspoken agreement, everyone had avoided discussing the case. Instead, there had been funny stories and lighthearted teasing.

Charlotte was nestled on Ryker's lap. When she'd fussed, bored with being in her highchair, he'd scooped her up so Hannah could continue eating. The baby looked so tiny against him. And happy. Ryker patiently rattled a toy for her amusement, and when the baby knocked it from the table, he picked it right back up. Hannah couldn't stop watching them. Even now, her gaze drifted in their direction.

What would it be like to have Ryker as a husband? She mentally gave herself a shake for even pondering the question. Hannah wasn't some schoolgirl with a crush, and one stolen moment was a far cry from a lifetime commitment. Their shared kiss had gone straight to her brain and hijacked her thoughts. But, oh, what a kiss. Her cheeks heated with the memory of it.

Ryker met her gaze across the table. Some hint of her secret thoughts must've been written in her expression, because his mouth tipped up in a heart-stopping grin. When her cheeks heated more, his smile widened, and he winked. She tore her gaze away from his under the pretense of wiping her hands on a napkin. From the corner of her eye, Hannah caught Ryker's mom watching her with a curious expression on her face. Then Zoe's gaze went to her son. A smile played on her lips.

Goodness. Had their exchange been noticed? It certainly seemed that way. Fear threatened to creep in, but Hannah refused to allow it. These feelings for Ryker felt good. It'd been a long time since she'd even thought about a man romantically. Maybe things would end with her heart broken, but right now, she didn't have the energy to fight these growing feelings.

"Mrs. Montgomery, you outdid yourself." Claire, dressed in her sheriff's uniform, pushed away from the table. "The food was fantastic, and I hate to break up the party, but I've got a to-do list that would make you weep. You won't mind if I steal some of your guests away for our meeting, will you?"

"Not at all." Zoe stood. "Y'all go on into the living room. I'll make coffee and bring in dessert."

Ryker's cousin, Walker, and his wife, Hayley, jumped up to clear the table. Jack stood and waved for Ryker to hand over Charlotte. The baby went willingly to his dad, her plump hand patting his weathered cheek. It seemed everyone in the Montgomery family had a way with kids.

Hannah went into the living room and took a seat on the couch. Ryker joined her, sitting close enough to brush her leg with his. The contact sent a bolt of electricity through her body. She leaned into the touch. Took comfort from it. Whatever news Claire and the others had to share, she wouldn't have to face what came next alone.

"Dusty Stillman is still missing." Gavin sat in an armchair before turning to face Hannah and Ryker. "But we've made significant progress in uncovering his connection to the Andersons. Eli and I"—he waved a finger between them—"interviewed everyone who worked for Thomas and Julie. Other than Lorrie, no one remembered seeing Dusty in the office. We confirmed Julie was acting strangely in the weeks before her murder. If you remember, at the time, we thought she'd uncovered Thomas's affair. Now we believe it was more serious than that."

"More serious?" Hannah frowned. "What do you mean?"

"Julie was writing fake prescriptions to factitious patients. Initially, we believed that was the connection to Dusty. He's a known drug dealer, after all. But further investigation proved that she wasn't the one entering the electronic prescriptions into the system and sending them to the pharmacy. It was done after hours. We can prove she was at social events or with her family during those times."

Ryker inhaled. "Thomas was using her name."

"Precisely." Eli leaned forward, placing his elbows on his knees. "Since Julie was a dentist, she could write narcotics prescriptions. She and her husband shared an office and staff. Thomas was smart enough to use her name in case the authorities figured out what was going on. We suspect that's what Julie uncovered before she was murdered. Looking through her computer history again, we noticed she was tracing the prescriptions. Times they were written. Pharmacies that were used. Julie was slowly putting the pieces together."

Hannah's mind whirled. "She was going to turn him in."

"I believe so." His gaze darkened. "Julie discovered her husband was having an affair, but she was pregnant and told multiple friends that she wanted to make the marriage work. But then she must've figured out Thomas was responsible for the fake prescriptions written in her name."

"Thomas could've told Dusty that Julie was on to them? She was digging around in the files for a while. He might've figured out she was suspicious. That could explain the confrontation between Thomas and Dusty in the parking lot a few weeks before the murder. Maybe Dusty threatened to hurt them both if Thomas didn't take care of the situation." Hannah inhaled. "Or he and Thomas planned her murder together. Could Dusty have stabbed her?"

"It's unlikely. Julie's killer, based on the angle and positioning of her wounds, was left-handed. Kristin's was right-handed. It's possible the same killer committed both crimes—a certain percentage of the population is ambidextrous—but it's more probable that we're looking at two different perpetrators."

"Thomas is left-handed," Ryker said. "That's another reason I suspected he'd killed Julie. Is Dusty right-handed?"

"His friends say he is."

Hannah rose and started pacing the length of the living room. "Okay, let's run through it from the beginning. Thomas uses his wife's name to write fake narcotic prescriptions. Dusty, a known drug dealer, pays him for every transaction and Thomas hides the money in a bookcase at his office. At some point, Julie realizes someone is writing fake prescriptions under her name. She becomes paranoid because she can't figure out which staff member it is. Then she discovers her husband is having an affair with his nurse, Lorrie. Suspicious, Julie digs in further and uncovers Thomas is also responsible for the fake prescriptions. That's the final straw. She confronts Thomas—or he figures out she's turning him into the police—and he kills her."

Eli nodded. "After Julie's murder, our investigation leads to Thomas. We arrest him. At first, he believes a talented lawyer will get him out of it. But as the trial gets closer, he becomes more desperate and enlists his old friend Dusty for help. They come up with a scheme to make it look like Julie's killer is still out there. The break-in at your house, the attack at the courthouse, and Kristin's murder are all connected. Each time Dusty screws up, he falls back and comes at it with a different approach."

Ryker leaned forward. "Can we prove Thomas and Dusty are communicating?"

"Unfortunately not." Claire rested her hands on her duty belt. "Thomas is under house arrest and wearing an electronic ankle monitor, so there's only so many places he can go. Court, his lawyer's office, and church. We got a search warrant for Thomas's house and tore it apart. We didn't find a burner phone. There haven't been any strange withdrawals from his bank accounts. Nothing to indicate he's paying Dusty or coordinating with him."

"My paralegal, Pam, suggested Thomas is too smart to risk communicating with Dusty directly," Hannah said. "I agree with her. I think he'd use a go-between. Initially, I suspected it was his girlfriend, Lorrie, but they broke up and she seemed genuinely remorseful about the affair."

"We looked into her." Gavin rolled his shoulders as if his back was bothering him. "She's telling the truth about the breakup. Both Lorrie and Thomas spoke to friends about it and haven't been seen together in public since. We also confirmed Lorrie was out of town working in San Diego when these recent attacks started. That doesn't mark her off the suspect list, but it lends credence to her statement."

Hannah began pacing again. "So if Lorrie isn't helping Thomas to communicate with Dusty, who is?"

Eli's mouth flattened. "It has to be someone Thomas trusts. He doesn't have family, which only leaves one logical possibility in my mind." He paused. "You won't like it, Hannah."

She turned to face him. "Who?"

TWENTY-ONE

The Law Offices of Jose Ortiz were strategically located in the center of three counties, with easy access to the freeway for anyone living in the wealthier Austin suburbs. The glass-and-chrome building glinted in the sunlight. Along with criminal law, the attorneys working for Jose handled probate, civil litigation, and family law.

Ryker took note of the expensive vehicles parked in the covered lot adjacent to the offices. "Looks like Jose pays his attorneys well. How long has he been in this location?"

"About five years." Eli steered his vehicle into a parking space and killed the engine. "He started with a prodigious law firm in Austin doing criminal defense work. That's his specialty. It's also where he was working when he handled Dusty Stillman's murder charge."

An interesting twist of events that left an unpleasant taste in Ryker's mouth. Why hadn't Jose recognized his own client from the courthouse surveillance video? Or from the sketch artist's rendering done right after Julie's murder? Eli hypothesized the oversight had been on purpose, that perhaps Jose was acting as Thomas's accomplice. Hannah hadn't agreed. She'd argued that Jose made so much money as an attorney, it would be foolish to risk his business and his reputation by conspiring with his client.

Ryker didn't know what to believe. Jose had given interviews to the media, making it clear the prosecution had no case against Thomas. How embarrassing would it be if he lost the trial? His reputation as a defense attorney would surely take a hit, but was that enough to join a conspiracy to commit murder? It felt like a reach. Then again, Ryker had worked cases with motives far less compelling.

He wanted to confront Jose with the information they had and gauge the attorney's reaction. Hannah had wanted to join them, but Ryker convinced her to stay on the ranch, under the protective guard of his dad and cousin. He couldn't keep her there forever. She had to go back to work tomorrow, but the less time Hannah spent off the ranch, the lower the chances of Dusty trying something.

Ryker prayed their efforts at finding the criminal would be successful. Claire was doing everything she could. An informant came forward late last night, claiming that Dusty had reached out. The criminal was attempting to garner support for another attack. What kind wasn't clear, but it terrified Ryker to know Dusty hadn't given up on killing Hannah.

Eli eyed him as they traversed the distance between the parking garage and the office building. "You're not gonna hulk out on me in there, are you? Jose might not have nice things to say about Hannah. I've gotten the feeling he doesn't particularly like her."

Surprise flickered through Ryker. He and Eli had worked dozens of cases together, and he'd never gotten an inkling that his friend didn't trust his abilities. "You think I can't handle myself?"

"I think you're developing feelings for Hannah and that can cloud your judgment. You practically punched out the District Attorney in the middle of the sheriff's department, remember?"

Oh, yeah. Ryker didn't like thinking about how Bruce had gotten in Hannah's face. The need to protect her had been instinctive and, in hindsight, indicated how deep his feelings for the gorgeous woman ran. Their kiss yesterday had rocked his world off its axis. He still wasn't sure what to do about this confusing mess he'd created. And now wasn't the time to worry about it.

He reached for the door handle. "I'll behave. Scout's honor."

Eli snorted. "You dropped out of Boy Scouts. Too many rules."

"And you went all the way to Eagle, cuz you love rules." Ryker grinned. "That's what makes us a good team. I know you'll keep me in line. You have since we were kids. Remember that time I nearly busted my head trying to dive into the lake off Gray's Rock?"

They'd been twelve. Eli had tossed a sack of marbles

over the edge of the cliff to illustrate just how dangerous jumping off would be. Ryker had taken one look at the crushed glass glittering on the rocks below and decided he didn't want to take the risk. Instead, they'd gone for ice cream.

The memory brought a broad smile to Eli's face. "You were a daredevil."

Ryker laughed. He had been. Somewhere along the way, after losing Alison and recognizing his own reckless behavior, he'd started playing it safe. Maybe too safe. He'd guarded his heart with a fierceness that prevented him from ever developing deep feelings for someone. And then Hannah came along. One look at her made him long to be the old Ryker. The one who threw caution to the wind and dared to defy the odds.

Fifteen minutes later, after introducing themselves to the receptionist and showing their badges, they were whisked to Jose's office on the top floor. Marble flooring, modern furniture, and touches of chrome gave the space an icy feel. In their blazers and boots, Ryker and Eli looked like misplaced cowboys.

Jose was stationed behind a lengthy desk made of the same marble as the flooring. He'd forgone a suit jacket, but his white button-up and tie were crisp. Diamond cufflinks winked from the end of his sleeve as he shook their hands. Pleasantries were exchanged. Jose offered them something to drink and then a seat in the visitor's chair facing his desk. Ryker settled in the wing-back that probably cost more than his entire year's salary.

"What can I help you with?" Jose asked, reclaiming his own seat behind the desk.

The attorney's position was elevated slightly. It wasn't enough that most people would notice, but Ryker recognized it as a power play. "We'd like to ask you about Dusty Stillman. As you know, we identified him as the man who assaulted Hannah in the courthouse."

Jose folded his hands. "Yes. He's likely the same criminal that threatened Thomas in the parking lot. And killed Julie."

"I'm surprised you didn't recognize him." Eli opened a leather case containing his tablet and removed an old arrest photograph, placing it on Jose's desk. "He was a client of yours. Seven years ago. Murder charges."

Jose's eyes widened slightly, but the move seemed calculated rather than one of genuine surprise. "Well, I've represented dozens of criminals over the years. I can't be expected to remember all of them." He glanced down at the picture. "Besides, Dusty didn't have that identifiable scar back then, as you can see from his booking photo."

"So you never suspected the criminal who attacked Hannah was someone you'd represented in the past?"

"Of course not. I want Dusty found more than anyone. Like I said, I believe he's responsible for Julie's murder. A crime my client has been falsely accused of."

"Dusty probably didn't kill Julie." Ryker kept his gaze locked on the defense attorney. "He's right-handed. Julie's killer was left-handed."

Jose arched a brow. "Excuse me, Ranger Montgomery, but that doesn't mean a thing. He could've hired someone to do it. Dusty is a known drug dealer and has been charged with murder before. I'm sure he has a host of misfit friends who'd be happy to aid in his criminal deeds."

An icy finger of trepidation touched the back of Ryker's neck. If Claire's informant was correct, Dusty had contacted some old friends for help to kill Hannah. Had he done the same with Julie? It wasn't outside the realm of possibility. But that didn't mean Thomas wasn't involved.

Ryker kept his tone even. "Our investigation has uncovered evidence that Thomas was using his wife's name to write narcotics prescriptions for fake patients. We believe that's where the money hidden in the bookcase in the office came from. Thomas and Dusty were working together. It's not a far cry to believe they conspired to kill Julie. And are now going after Hannah."

"Those are serious accusations." Jose was nonplussed. He leaned back into his chair casually. "Can you prove my client has had contact with Dusty? Or that Thomas was running a drug scheme?"

"The investigation is still early. It's possible Thomas is using a go-between to communicate with Dusty."

Jose's gaze narrowed as his mouth hardened. "Are you accusing me of something, Ranger Montgomery?"

"No, sir. My colleague and I merely wanted to ask why you didn't recognize Dusty from the courthouse surveillance footage. It seemed odd that you'd defended Dusty against serious murder charges, but never mentioned it to anyone in law enforcement even when his name was released to the media."

"There's no mystery to it. I merely forgot." Jose glanced at his watch, hit a button discreetly placed on his desk, and then rose from his chair. "You'll have to forgive me, gentlemen, but I have another meeting to attend. Please keep me informed about the progress of your case."

The secretary appeared seemingly out of nowhere. Ryker and Eli followed her back to the elevator. Before the doors closed, Ryker caught a glimpse of Jose speaking on his cell phone. His expression was pinched. Despite his calm demeanor, their questions had rattled him.

Ryker didn't believe for one minute that Jose hadn't recognized Dusty from the surveillance video. He'd purposefully hidden his connection to the criminal. Worse, he'd known Dusty's name but hadn't shared it with law enforcement. They'd lost days in their investigation trying to learn who "Cash" was.

Why had Jose lied? Was it because he was protecting Thomas? His client had been running a million-dollar drug scheme. They'd traced it back years. It's possible Thomas wasn't the only doctor involved. The entire thing could be part of a bigger network.

What had they stumbled into?

And was Jose a part of it?

TWENTY-TWO

"Thank you for taking the time to see me." Julie's mother, Mandy Jackson, wrapped her fingers around the mug of tea Hannah placed in front of her. Her gray hair was swept back from a face lined with exhaustion and grief. "I've been following the developments in the news. I'm very sorry about the lawyer from your office. The one that was murdered. Kristin. That was her name, right?"

"Yes." Hannah pulled out a chair across from the other woman. A pang of sadness hit her at the mention of Kristin's name. The young woman hadn't deserved to be terrorized by a murderer. "Kristin Michaels. Her family is from San Marcos. That's where the funeral will be."

"Her poor parents." Mandy swallowed hard. "I know all too well what they're going through."

"I know you do."

Mandy had called an hour ago requesting a meeting. Normally, Hannah wouldn't have invited Julie's mom to the ranch, but given the threats, it seemed like the best option. It was also an opportunity. Mandy and her daughter had been close and their family dinners had often included Thomas. They'd spent holidays and vacations together. Mandy had known her son-in-law well.

Hannah needed additional names of individuals Thomas might've roped into his drug scheme. She wasn't convinced Jose was involved. Too risky. The rangers were doing a deep dive into his background, but other than representing Dusty seven years ago, there were no other obvious connections.

Ryker set a plate of cookies in the center of the table before pulling out his own chair. He looked stressed. His hair was rumpled, as if he'd been running his hands through it, and faint lines bracketed his mouth. After interviewing Jose, he'd come back to the ranch, and they'd worked for hours following various leads. None had brought them any closer to figuring out who Thomas was using as a go-between.

Not even questioning Lorrie had yielded any new results. She'd been forthcoming with information, but because of the clandestine nature of her relationship with Thomas, hadn't been introduced to any of his friends. The young woman had known little about the man she'd had an affair with.

"I won't beat around the bush, Hannah." Mandy straightened her shoulders and drew a breath in between her teeth. "I've heard news reports that the charges against Thomas will be dropped soon. Perhaps as soon as tomorrow morning. Is that true?"

"No. The investigation is still ongoing. I don't want to decide until we are closer to trial."

"Have you talked to your boss about that?"

Hannah frowned. Her last conversation with Bruce hadn't been cordial. He'd called shortly after Kristin's murder, and once again, clarified that he wanted the charges against Thomas dropped. A sinking feeling settled in the pit of her stomach. Was Bruce planning to drop the charges without telling her first?

No. Surely not. Her boss was politically savvy and was facing increasing pressure over this case, but he'd never make a decision without informing her about it first.

Hannah shared a glance with Ryker before turning back to Mandy. "I haven't recently, but he knows what my feelings are." She reached across and placed a hand on the other woman's sleeve. "Be careful about listening to news reports. The reporters can exaggerate and over-analyze every nugget of information."

"I know." She twisted the mug between her hands. "I just... you're aware Thomas and Bruce were good friends."

"Of course. He's told me." It was a good segue to the questions Hannah wanted to ask, so she took it. "How much do you know about Thomas's friends?"

Mandy shrugged. "He's popular. Or was popular before Julie's murder. Lots of political events, which is how he and Bruce connected. Thomas liked money. I never understood why he became a small-town doctor when he could've made two or three times the income working for a major hospital. I suppose Julie had a lot to do with it. She convinced him it was easier to have power and influence in a small town. Of course, my daughter used her connections to raise money for charity. Thomas..." Her gaze drifted off. "He was shallow. He wanted people to notice him when he walked into a room."

It wasn't the first time someone had mentioned that trait. Hannah had heard it several times from Julie's friends. "I know this has come up before, but I need to ask again. Can you think of anyone Thomas was close to?"

"No. He was a user. Thomas liked you, but only if he could get something from you. He didn't have any real friends."

Ryker leaned forward. "What about his attorney, Jose? What was their relationship like before all of this happened?"

Mandy shrugged again. "Good, I suppose. Come to think of it, Thomas, Jose, and Bruce used to travel together from time to time. They all liked deep sea fishing. They'd take their wives too. I remember Julie talking about how sick she got on the boat once. It was upsetting because Thomas didn't seem to care." Her mouth pursed. "I kept my mouth shut. Julie would tell me these stories and I'd be fuming, but didn't say a word. He was her husband, and several of my friends warned me that keeping the peace with my son-in-law was better for the family. Why on earth did I listen to them?"

"Because your daughter was a grown woman capable

of making her own choices." Hannah hated hearing the grief and regret buried in Mandy's voice. "You did what you thought was best for her. Hindsight is always twenty-twenty."

She wiped a tear from her cheek. "I still blame myself. That won't change."

"I hope someday it will." Once again, Hannah placed a hand on the older woman's arm. "Julie wouldn't want you to stay sad for the rest of your life. If there's anything I've learned while working this case, it's how much your daughter loved you. She'd want you to be happy."

Mandy breathed out and patted Hannah's hand. "Thank you for saying that, dear. And for everything you're doing to get justice for Julie." She offered Ryker a watery smile. "You too, Ranger Montgomery. No matter what happens, I know you both did your best. You will always be in my prayers."

Hannah's chest tightened. She was touched beyond words. From the look on Ryker's face, so was he.

Together, they walked Mandy out to her car. She drove off, her headlights winking in the darkness before disappearing. A faint breeze lifted the strands of Hannah's hair and crickets resumed chirping. Oliver, the ranch dog, nudged her hand, looking for a pat. She obliged him by giving an ear rub.

"Did you know Bruce, Jose, and Thomas used to go on fishing trips together?" Ryker asked.

"No, but the news doesn't surprise me. Bruce owns a boat and often entertains on it. I've been invited a time or two, although I haven't gone. Since Thomas and Jose donated to Bruce's campaign during the election for District Attorney, it seems reasonable he'd invite them for some deep sea fishing."

Ryker grunted. "It's a thread to pull anyway."

Shock vibrated through her. "You can't believe Jose and Bruce are both part of Thomas's drug scheme? That's... ridiculous." She turned toward him, hands planted on her hips. "Not everyone is a criminal."

"Maybe not, but I won't eliminate someone just because the person is a respected member of the community." He pointed down the road. "Do you think Mandy imagined her daughter would be murdered, let alone by her own son-in-law?"

"Of course not, but—"

"There is no but. Don't you get it? Whoever is behind this won't stop until you're dead. I'll do anything to prevent that from happening, even if it means taking a hard look at every person in Thomas Anderson's life. I don't care that Bruce is the District Attorney. If he has something to do with this, then I'll take him down."

Hannah opened her mouth, but the words died on her tongue. Ryker was right. They couldn't eliminate anyone as a suspect. Nor should they. It would be a disservice to the oath they took to uphold the law fairly and equally. But she also recognized that a huge part of what was fueling Ryker was fear.

He didn't want anything bad to happen to her.

Problem was, he didn't control that. She didn't either. Both of them could do everything right, and still things might go badly. Ultimately, God was in charge. They had to put their faith in His divine wisdom.

Hannah stepped forward and wrapped her arms around his waist. He was rigid for a moment and then relaxed into her touch. She laid her head on his chest, taking comfort in the steady beat of his heart. "I know you want to protect me, but there are some things outside of your control. We can't guarantee Thomas will be brought to justice for killing Julie. Or that we'll catch Dusty. Our best is all we can offer."

Ryker sighed long and low. "I have trouble accepting that. Our limitations, I mean."

"I know." Hannah tilted her head up and brushed her lips across his. "Prayer might help."

He nodded. Then Ryker cupped her cheek, the warmth of his palm sending a delicious wave of heat through her. The rough pad of his thumb trailed across her bottom lip. Desire tangled with worry in his eyes. He cared about her. Hannah felt that down to her bones, but their relationship would fail before it started if fear got in the way. She refused to step back. Ryker was working through his issues. She'd give him the opportunity.

He tilted his head and captured her lips. Hannah's heart kicked into high gear as her hands rose along his broad chest before lifting to his neck. Her fingers threaded into the soft strands of hair at his nape. Everything about this man pulled her closer. His bravery. His caring. The way he loved his family and tried so hard to do the right thing. The kiss deepened, stealing the last of her breath.

A piercing beep broke the intimate moment. Ryker immediately stiffened and pulled away, but kept one hand on Hannah's arm. Cold night air replaced the warmth of their embrace. He yanked his cell phone from his pocket. The intensity in his expression sent a river of worry arcing through her.

She shivered. "What is it?"

"Get into the house. Now." Ryker pulled her toward the front door. "Someone's breached our security system."

TWENTY-THREE

Ryker had planned for this contingency, but that didn't make him feel any better. Worry spiked as he led Hannah through the front door and toward her bedroom. Charlotte was sleeping peacefully in the crib. So innocent and sweet in her pajamas. Completely unaware that a killer— or killers—were heading their way. Ryker gently scooped her up. The weight of the baby in his arms added a new load of responsibility to his shoulders. He couldn't let anything happen to this precious child or her aunt.

He handed Charlotte to Hannah, his movements smooth despite the adrenaline coursing through his veins. Hannah pressed the baby to her chest. Zoe appeared in the doorway. His mom had been preparing dinner. An apron was tied around her waist and flour streaked across one cheek. In her hands, she carried a shotgun.

"Get in the closet." Ryker hustled Hannah into the large walk-in. It was an interior room with no windows, which would prevent anyone from breaching the space serendipitously. He didn't plan on letting Dusty get that close, but every layer of protection helped. Ryker pointed to the doorknob he'd replaced the day after Hannah's arrival. "There's a lock on this. Use it."

Hannah's complexion was pale, but she kept control of her emotions. "I need Charlotte's diaper bag."

"Got it." Zoe entered the closet, still carrying the shotgun, with the bag slung over one shoulder. She met Ryker's gaze. "Your father is in the office. He's accessing the cameras on the property."

Ryker gave a sharp nod. He started to step out of the closet when Hannah snagged his hand.

Their gazes met. Ryker's chest tightened at the emotions written in her gorgeous blue eyes. She was terrified about what would happen next, but there was also acceptance. A trust. In him and in God. The power of that faith reached inside Ryker and grabbed hold of his heart.

He was falling in love with her. Utterly and completely. And once this threat was neutralized, he intended to do whatever was necessary to handle the baggage holding him back from stepping forward into the future with her.

Ryker kissed Hannah's forehead before gently touching Charlotte's back. "It's going to be okay. Stay here with my mom and don't open that door up for anyone except me or my father."

Before she could reply, he pulled away and shut the closet door behind him. The lock snicked into place.

Resolve and a fierce need to protect his family fueled his steps to the office space near the living room. His father was positioned behind the computer. Another shotgun rested across his lap. Oliver stood at attention next to the balcony doors. The dog's body language was tense, as if he was also ready to defend his home.

Layers and layers of protection. Ryker prayed the precautions he'd put in place were enough.

"Two individuals on the southeast corner of the property." Jack accessed the camera footage and hit play. His expression was grim. "They're armed. Rifles."

Ryker watched as two figures dressed in black clothes and wearing ski masks crept across the perimeter of the property carrying semiautomatic rifles. They'd gotten reports that Dusty had been reaching out to friends, trying to garner help. Seemed he finally found someone. "Did you call 911?"

Jack nodded. "Deputies are en route. Estimated time is about fifteen minutes. Walker and Hayley are still running errands in town, but Eli is in the barn saddling up horses."

It was a stroke of good fortune that Ryker's colleague was on the ranch during the attack, especially since his cousin had gone into town. Eli had come to the ranch to have dinner with the family and then go over the case. His presence meant that Ryker had a fighting chance to capture Dusty tonight.

He clapped a hand on his shoulder. "Call dispatch back and let them know that Eli and I are on location.

Then keep watching the cameras. Text me if anything changes."

Before his father could reply, Ryker turned on his heel. He slipped out of the house into the cool night air. Motion detection lights flicked on as he raced to the barn. As his father said, Eli had already saddled two horses. The ones he'd chosen were steady but fast. Rifles, taken from the locked gun room, were nestled in the scabbards. Ryker sent up a silent prayer that his childhood friend still spent enough time at the ranch to know where all the equipment was kept.

Eli handed him the reins to a black gelding. "Did you see the footage?"

"Yep." Ryker swung himself into the saddle. "Intruders are armed. There were two on camera, but I don't want to assume more aren't out there. The south-east corner is mostly wooded."

"I'm in text communication with Gavin who is coordinating the deputies. I've instructed him to send one responding unit to the main house and the other one to the dirt road running along the far side of the property. We can flank Dusty and his friend. Capture them tonight and end this thing."

It was a good plan. Ryker nodded. "Let's do it."

Fresh adrenaline shot through his veins as Ryker gave a gentle kick to his horse's flanks. The gelding needed very little encouragement. He bolted from the barn. His hooves tore chunks in the grass as they crossed the fields toward the woods surrounding the property. Moonlight coated the trees in a silvery glow. Ryker tugged on the reins to slow the horse down as they approached the southeast corner. Goosebumps broke out across his skin.

He pulled his weapon from the holster on his belt. Eli stationed himself thirty yards away. Ryker was too far to see his face, but his fellow lawman braced the rifle against his shoulder. They would stay on the horses for the time being. The elevated position would give them a height advantage and make traversing the dense woods easier. It could also place them in danger since they would be bigger targets to the enemy. Ryker sent up a silent prayer that he was making the right decision.

He hooted like an owl. A signal from their childhood days. He and Eli had spent many hours playing in these woods. They knew every square inch of it. The intruders' entry point was about two miles in front of them. Provided they stayed on a direct path heading for the house and didn't get lost in the woods, Dusty and his friend should be close by.

Ryker and Eli would encircle the men. Deputies would block their escape via the dirt road.

Hannah and Charlotte would be safe.

Tree branches tugged at his clothes as Ryker urged his horse past the tree line. The black gelding was sure-footed, handling the roots and underbrush with ease. Darkness cast long shadows big enough to hide a man in. Eli wasn't visible, but the gentle sound of his horse walking through the woods carried across the distance between them. Ryker adjusted the hold on his weapon. His heart picked up speed and his vision threatened to narrow. He took a deep breath to counteract the effects of the adrenaline.

The faint rustle of movement caught his attention. Ryker pulled on the reins, bringing his horse to a halt. He peered into the brush. A branch shifted, followed by a muttered curse. Then silence.

Someone was there. But just one person. Where was the second intruder? Had they split up?

Silently, Ryker slipped from the saddle. His boots sank into the leaves and pine needles covering the forest floor. He debated announcing his presence and ordering the criminal to freeze, but the man was armed. With a semiautomatic. The last thing Ryker wanted was a potential shootout in the woods. The best option was to sneak up on whoever it was, disarm the man, and arrest him.

He crept forward, gun leading the way. A man-sized shadow came into view. His rifle was propped up against a tree and he was adjusting the zipper on his pants. Ryker took advantage of the situation without a second thought. He pointed his weapon.

"Police!" His tone was hard. "Put your hands up."

The man froze. For half a heartbeat, Ryker feared the criminal would ignore the order. Then the intruder raised his hands in the air. Excellent decision.

With another few orders, Ryker had the man down on the ground with his hands on the back of his head. He paused, unable to cuff the criminal without holstering his gun. He placed a knee squarely on the man's back, ensuring he was planted on the ground, and then reached for his cuffs. Pulse pounding, he holstered his weapon.

Like a lightning strike, the criminal shifted his body to the left. A blade flashed. Ryker deflected the knife thrust and slammed the heel of his hand into the other man's face. Cartilage crumpled. The guy screamed as blood spurted from his nose.

Without wasting a second, Ryker caught the hand with the knife and twisted it hard. The blade fell to the ground. It was tiny and had probably been hidden in the man's shirtsleeve. Pulse pounding and breath quick, Ryker cuffed his attacker before the guy could recover from the pain of having his nose broken.

"Where's your friend?" Ryker patted the criminal down, searching for any other weapons. "The one you came with."

"You think I'm gonna tell you anything? You broke my nose!"

"If you're looking for sympathy, call your mama." Ryker spun the criminal around and ripped off his ski mask. The man staring back at him had a beard and beady eyes. Not Dusty. "I'm a Texas Ranger and this is my property. You know what that means? You're in serious trouble. So unless you plan on spending the rest of your life in prison, I suggest you answer my questions. Where is your friend?"

The intruder sagged. "Which one? There are three of us."

That news sent Ryker's heart skyrocketing in his chest. His gaze shot to the woods. Eli was armed and careful, but he only knew about two intruders.

Ryker yanked out his cell phone and quickly shot off

a text to his fellow ranger. Sirens from approaching deputies blared through the night air. Backup was close. "Where are the other two?"

"One's in the getaway car. The other isn't far. I came to take a leak—"

Gunshots erupted in the woods.

TWENTY-FOUR

The hospital waiting room was packed with people. Hannah slipped some coins into a coffee machine and waited until the dark brew finished filling the cup before lifting it into her hand. Exhaustion clouded her thoughts. It was nearing one in the morning, and Eli had been in surgery for hours. He'd suffered from two gunshot wounds to the abdomen. By the time he got to the hospital, he'd lost so much blood, the doctors warned he might not make it through the operation.

Ryker sat on the far side of the room, slumped in a plastic chair, with his head in his hands. Dried blood stained his shirt. Several members of Company A were also there, along with their wives. Hannah discovered they—along with Ryker's parents—were Eli's only family. His father left when he was three, his mother died in a car crash when Eli was in college. His younger brother was in prison. Drugs.

Hannah crossed the room and placed a hand on

Ryker's back. The muscles under her palm were rigid. He lifted his head, his eyes filled with worry. It punched a hole right through her heart. For all his bravado, Ryker's emotional well ran deep. No wonder he'd built so many walls around his heart. When he cared, he was all in. Hannah had quickly discovered that Ryker didn't do anything by half-measures.

She handed him the coffee. "Here. Take this and I'll get you something to eat."

"I don't want anything." His gaze drifted to the doors leading to the emergency room as he set the drink down on the table next to his chair. Then he took her hand between his. "How much longer can the surgery take? It's been hours."

She leaned against his shoulder, resting her other hand in the crook of his elbow. "As long as it needs to take. No news isn't bad. It means the doctors are being thorough, so Eli has the best chance of recovery." Hannah didn't want to give false promises. Eli's condition was grave, but he was also young and strong. "All we can do is wait. And pray."

He blew out a breath. "I said more prayers in the last week than I have in my whole life." His jaw tightened and tears shimmered in his eyes. "Sometimes it feels like God isn't listening."

Before Hannah could answer, the doors leading to the emergency room swished open. Her heart leapt into her throat, but then Claire and Gavin emerged. The couple wore grim expressions. Gavin greeted a few members of Company A while his wife crossed the room heading for Hannah and Ryker. Her sheriff's uniform was mud spattered from traipsing through the woods on the Montgomery property and her ponytail was askew.

Claire had been one of the first people at the ranch after receiving the 911 call from Ryker's dad. She, along with Gavin, were leading the investigation.

Hannah rose. "What's going on?"

"The perpetrator who exchanged gunfire with Eli didn't make it. He died in the ambulance. We've identified him as 18-year-old Larry Higgins. He's got a juvenile record, but there's no obvious connection to Dusty. My deputies did spot a Chevy truck fleeing the scene, and they gave chase, but the driver escaped."

"What about the man I arrested?" Ryker asked.

"Simon Harper. His nose is broken, but otherwise he's unharmed. He and Dusty go way back. They were arrested together during a robbery almost twenty years ago. I've questioned Simon, but he refuses to talk without a deal of immunity." Claire's nose wrinkled. "Normally, I would never concede to that kind of demand at this point in the investigation, but given that Dusty was probably driving the getaway car and is still at large, it's worth considering."

Hannah agreed. "Have you contacted Bruce?"

"I have. He's on his way. Bruce will handle the immunity deal, but would like for you to join us when we question Simon." Claire cast an apologetic look toward Ryker. "You'll have to stay here. Simon claimed police brutality. Internal Affairs has to do an investigation, which means you're on the sidelines until they clear you."

He rolled his eyes. "Fantastic."

Bruce strolled into the waiting room. Despite the early-morning hour, he wore a three-piece suit complete with a tie. His hair was damp, as if he'd recently showered, and his jaw was clean-shaven. Bags created deep grooves in the area under his eyes. He looked annoyed at being dragged out of bed, but Hannah knew he wouldn't let anyone else handle this immunity deal. Not with the stakes being this high.

"We'd better go." Claire waved at Bruce and then turned back to Hannah. "Word of warning, Simon's attorney is Jose Ortiz."

Ryker's jaw clenched. "Isn't that convenient?"

Claire shrugged. "I agree it's suspicious, but Jose has represented Simon many times over the years. We don't have any evidence linking this crime to Thomas Anderson, so there's no obvious conflict of interest. Simon is entitled to representation. There's nothing to prevent him from choosing Jose."

She moved away to snag Gavin from his conversation with Lieutenant Rodriguez. Hannah took a step toward Bruce, but Ryker grabbed her hand, halting her forward momentum.

"Be careful, Hannah. I don't like the idea of Bruce and Jose being involved in whatever statement Simon is about to make." He leaned forward. "Stay close to Claire and Gavin. Don't leave their sight."

A shiver of dread coursed down her spine. Her gaze skipped over the waiting room, snagging on Charlotte, who was held by Ryker's dad. Her little head rested on

Jack's chest. Zoe had wrapped a blanket around the baby to keep her warm. The diaper bag rested at her feet.

At any other time, the sight would have brought a smile to Hannah's face. The Montgomerys looked like a set of doting grandparents. But Ryker's warning stole her breath. She met his gaze. "You think Dusty might attack again?"

"Not immediately, but we also don't know who we can trust. Simon is working with Dusty. Dusty is working with Thomas. Bruce and Jose are both friends with Thomas, and right now, we can't eliminate them as suspects." He trailed a hand over her hair, the touch tender and loving. "Just... be careful, okay?"

"I will."

Ryker was probably being overly cautious. It was his nature to be suspicious of everyone, but Hannah still wasn't convinced that anyone else was involved in Thomas's drug scheme. Hopefully, whatever Simon had to say would lead them to Dusty and this entire nightmare could be over.

She followed Claire and Gavin into the emergency room and down the hall. Simon, his nose bandaged and face swollen, sat in a bed with a dark look on his face. Jose greeted Hannah with a slick smile that twisted her insides. She didn't know if Ryker's warning was coloring her thoughts, but the attorney resembled a cat with the mouse before he went in for the kill.

The next few minutes were spent dealing with paperwork and clarifying the terms of the immunity deal. Bruce clarified that nothing would officially happen until they heard what Simon had to say. If the criminal offered them useful information that led to the capture of Dusty, then they would reduce the charges to a misdemeanor trespassing.

Hannah wasn't thrilled about letting Simon go with a slap on the wrist. But sometimes deals had to be made. Dusty was a danger to the public. He'd murdered a fellow prosecutor. They needed to get him off the streets.

Once the paperwork was signed, Bruce turned a steely gaze on Simon. "Where is Dusty Stillman?"

"I don't know exactly where he is. Dusty moves around a lot." Simon gestured for Jose to give him paper and a pen. His voice was muffled thanks to his broken nose. "I'll write the hideouts I know about. If you search, you'll find him. I can also give you the names of some people he deals with. Just make sure you catch him, otherwise he'll come after me, and believe me, you don't want to be on Dusty's bad side."

"Tell them about what Dusty told you yesterday," Jose urged.

"He contacted me last night and said he had a job for me. We met up at this dive bar across town. Dusty's given me work before. Robberies and drug deals. That kind of thing. Anyway, he said we were gonna make a fortune together by robbing a ranch owned by wealthy people. Everyone would be gone. Easy money."

Hannah frowned. That made little sense. Why would Dusty hire two men to break onto the Montgomery ranch?

Gavin must've thought the same thing because he

interjected. "Hold on. You were just supposed to rob the place. Nothing else?"

Simon nodded. "Yeah, man. I'm not a saint, but there are some things I don't get involved in. Dusty lied to me about who owned the ranch. He never mentioned it belonged to a Texas Ranger. And I sure wouldn't have involved Larry in this mess had I known the truth." He swallowed hard. "He was just a kid."

His remorse and grief seemed genuine. Hannah couldn't make sense of this new information. She had the feeling there was some kind of ulterior motive. That suspicion was confirmed when Jose leaned forward and said, "Explain what else Dusty told you at the bar last night?"

"Oh yeah. The TV was on, and the news was talking about that attorney who'd been killed. The prosecutor."

"Kristin Michaels." Bruce pursed his lips. "Go on."

"Yeah, that one." Simon handed Claire the pad on which he'd scribbled down the information about Dusty. She quietly slipped from the room. "Dusty said he was the one that killed her. He was laughing about it, saying the police didn't know who was behind it all. Then he told me he murdered that doctor's wife last year."

"Julie Anderson?" Bruce asked.

"Yeah, I think that was her name. Apparently she and Dusty were in the drug business together, but she double-crossed him. Dusty killed her for it. He even showed me the knife he used."

Jose arched his brows as his gaze swung to Bruce. The two men shared some kind of secret look.

Hannah's gut clenched. She believed that Ryker might be right and there was far more going on than they knew. She narrowed her gaze at the man on the bed. "You expect us to believe that Dusty just offered this information up? Why would he do that?"

"Dusty is a bragger. He likes to talk about the stuff he did."

"And it didn't make you nervous to commit a robbery with a killer?"

Simon shrugged. "I knew he'd killed before. As long as I wasn't involved in the murders, I didn't care."

Unbelievable. Hannah had heard a lot of things during her time as a prosecutor, but this had to be one of the biggest coincidences she'd ever come across. She opened her mouth to ask another question, but Bruce cut her off with a look.

"ADA Lawson, could I have a word?"

Her boss marched to the door and out into the hall. He kept walking until they were around the corner. This section of the emergency room was next to a supply closet and the bathroom. A bit more secluded, which is probably what Bruce was looking for since he was about to tear into her, judging from the stormy expression on his face.

She didn't give him a chance. "We need to be careful here, Bruce. I don't think Simon is lying, but I do believe Dusty weaved a tall tale and then sent him onto the Montgomery property knowing he'd probably be caught by the police. This is some kind of setup."

"Why on earth would Dusty confess to a murder he didn't commit?" Bruce scowled. "That's absurd."

"Not if he's working with Thomas." She frowned. "Simon's story doesn't even make sense. Dusty couldn't have killed Julie. He's right-handed and her murderer was left-handed."

"That's not conclusive and you know it. Dusty could've had an injury on his right hand, forcing him to use his left. We can't ignore Simon's statement just because you don't like what he's saying."

"I'm not suggesting we ignore it. I'm merely saying we need to be careful in accepting his statement as the truth."

Bruce gave her a sympathetic look. "You've been through a lot the last few days. I know this case is weighing on you, but this isn't the way to handle it. You need to accept that Thomas Anderson is probably innocent of his wife's murder."

"Maybe, but I think we should reserve judgment until all the facts are in. If you drop the charges against Thomas now, and then have to bring them again, it'll be a mess. We're close to uncovering the truth. Give it a bit more time."

He hesitated and then sighed. "I'll wait until Dusty is found and interviewed, but if we continue to discover evidence that proves he's responsible for Julie's murder, then the charges against Thomas will be dropped."

She could hardly argue with that logic. Hannah didn't want an innocent man charged with a crime he didn't commit. But Bruce's quick concession surprised her. He'd been adamant about dropping the charges against Thomas the last several times they'd discussed the matter.

He arched a brow as if reading her thoughts. "Don't look so shocked. This isn't the first time I've deferred to your judgment and given you additional time."

"I know, but this attitude is a switch from the last few conversations we've had."

"You have Pam to thank for that."

Her paralegal? Hannah's brow crinkled in confusion.

A sheepish look came over Bruce's face. "She overheard my end of the conversation we had right after Kristin was murdered. I was... upset and took my emotions out on you. Pam gently reminded me that you operate with honesty and integrity. You'd never pursue anything just to be stubborn. Nor are you angling to purposefully hurt me with my constituents." He closed his eyes and shook his head. "I've spent too much time with politicians. Always looking over my shoulder waiting for someone to try and take me down. I'm sorry. I should've listened to what you had to say with a more open mind."

His apology touched her. Hannah immediately regretted her suspicions of him. "I'm sorry too. This case has been hard on everyone and Kristin's murder was a blow. I could've been more patient with you."

"Water under the bridge. Let's focus on catching Dusty and figuring out who is responsible for Julie's murder."

"Yes, sir."

With a final nod, Bruce went past her and around the corner. Hannah waited until he was out of view before sagging against the wall. Maybe her boss was right. With everything going on, she might not be seeing this case clearly. Hannah had been wrong about Bruce's intentions. Maybe she was wrong about Thomas too.

She pressed her thumb and index finger to the bridge of her nose. A migraine was forming along her temples. Not surprising considering the depth of her stress and emotional exhaustion. Some cold water on her face and neck would help.

Hannah slipped into the bathroom. Flipping on the tap, she let the water run until it was icy, and then cupped her hands to gather it. She splashed it on her face. Water dripped off her chin as she eyed her reflection. Her eyes were bloodshot and her neck ached from the tension in her muscles. She ducked her head to douse her face with more cold water.

The door to the bathroom creaked open. Embarrassed, Hannah quickly reached for the paper towel dispenser. It was silly, but she didn't want a stranger to see her splashing around in the sink like a baby bird. She swiped at water gathering on her chin. Movement in the mirror drew her gaze to the person behind her.

She gasped.

Dusty, wearing hospital scrubs, moved quicker than a snake. He punched her. Pain exploded as her body tumbled into the wall next to the sink. She fell to the ground. Stars floated past her vision. Before she could blink them away, Dusty was on top of her. One meaty hand clamped over her mouth and then something jabbed her neck.

Her vision blurred. Hannah struggled, but her movements became weaker and weaker until her mind couldn't connect to her limbs. He'd drugged her. The thought floated somewhere in the back of her brain, cutting through the panic, and then she was on a cloud. Drifting. Drifting.

No. Dusty was carrying her. He set her down on a mattress. A mask covered the lower half of his face. Then she was moving again. Being wheeled someplace. Past the nurses' station. Hannah desperately tried to cry out, but she couldn't get her voice to work. This couldn't be happening. Blackness crowded the edges of her vision.

Hannah fought it. She needed to stay awake. Needed to fight.

Another voice. Familiar, but she couldn't place it. Once again, Dusty's face hovered above hers. His dark eyes were triumphant. He was going to kill her. Once again, she tried to cry out. Willed her tongue to move, but it refused.

Then everything went dark.

TWENTY-FIVE

Ryker paced the length of the waiting room, rocking Charlotte back to sleep. She'd woken and had a bottle, but then couldn't settle. He sympathized. His nerves were also frayed, and the minutes ticked by slowly. Still no word from the doctors about Eli. Gavin, Claire, and Hannah hadn't come back yet either. Ryker was tempted to march himself into the emergency room and demanded an update. Sheer willpower held him back.

Charlotte whimpered. Ryker sensed she was powering up for a big cry, so he changed tactics and began swaying back and forth like a swing. "It's okay, sweetheart. Your aunt will be back soon."

She blinked giant blue eyes at him. Their color was the same shade as Hannah's. Charlotte wasn't her daughter, but for a moment, Ryker wondered what it would be like to have children with her. The thought sent a mixture of hope and terror running through him in equal measure.

"You're good with her." Zoe smiled softly from a nearby chair. She was nursing a cup of coffee.

His dad was dozing a short distance away. Several members of Company A were scattered about. Some were talking in low tones. Others were simply sitting in front of the television. All of them were anxiously awaiting news about Eli.

Ryker kept swaying. Charlotte's eyes drifted shut. He ran a hand over a wayward curl, smoothing it down. "She's a calm baby. Not like Travis." His youngest cousin had stayed with them shortly after having her own child. "That kid screamed for four months straight."

Zoe chuckled. "He had colic." The smile on her face faded as she studied him. "You're falling in love with Hannah, aren't you?"

The question caught him off guard, but Ryker shouldn't have been surprised. His mother could read him like a book and often knew his feelings better than he did. Zoe rarely interfered in his love life though. Of course, Hannah had been living with them for the last several days. She and his mom had bonded.

"Yes. I'm falling in love with her." It was a relief to say the words out loud, and suddenly, Ryker wanted to spill every tangled thought running through his mind. "And I don't know what to do about it. The thought of losing her is terrifying me. After what happened to Alison... it's too much, Mom. I can't take it."

"Because you still blame yourself for what happened to Alison?"

"In part." He struggled to sort through his emotions.

"But I don't think that's all of it. It's the lack of control. The pain that comes when you lose someone you care about."

He glanced down at Charlotte. Long lashes rested on plump cheeks and her breathing was deep and steady.

Ryker stopped swaying and took a seat next to his mom. "Eli is one of the best lawmen I know. He does everything by the book, follows every rule. And still he got shot." Hot tears pricked his eyes as the memory of finding his childhood friend lying on the ground bleeding out flashed in his mind. Ryker battled them back. "Going through what I am right now, with Eli in surgery, is too hard. And he's just my friend. He's not my wife or the mother of my children. I can't see myself doing it, Mom."

She was quiet for a long moment. Then she sighed. "You were young when your father passed away, so you don't remember how he and I were as a couple. We were passionately in love. Cal swept me off my feet with his charming smile and kind heart. When he died..." She inhaled sharply and let it out slowly. "I fell apart completely. Couldn't get out of bed for weeks. I thought that part of my life was over for good. And it was. Until I met Jack."

Her gaze drifted to her husband. "I was terrified to fall in love with him, Ryker. Terrified. But then I realized something very important." She turned back to face him. "My life was greater with Cal in it. No matter how painful it was to lose him, if I'd closed myself off to his love, that would have been the genuine tragedy."

Her words rang with wisdom. Would it have been

better if Hannah had never come into his life? Ryker couldn't imagine it. He didn't want to. She'd entered his world and opened his eyes to the kind of love he hadn't known was possible.

"I know losing Alison affected you deeply," Zoe continued. "Childhood traumas have a way of sinking their claws into us in a powerful way." She laid a hand on his arm. "But you were never to blame for her death. Punishing yourself by rejecting Hannah doesn't do anyone any good."

Is that what he was doing? Punishing himself?

The truth hit him like a smack in the face. That's exactly what he was doing. Yes, there was an aspect of self-protection, but it'd gotten muddled with the true source of his problem. Surrender. Accepting that, ultimately, God was in control.

Ryker didn't want to acknowledge that he'd done his best and Alison died anyway. It made him feel weak. Out of control. So he'd punished himself for something that was never his fault. Hannah had recognized it, tried to explain the fallacy of his thoughts, but he hadn't truly listened to her. He hadn't been ready.

Now he was. Ryker wanted to rid himself of the burden he'd been carrying around since Alison died.

God, I turn to you with an open heart and new understanding. All this time, I've been asking for repentance, but there was never anything to forgive. You've been trying to tell me that for years, but especially so in the last week. First the conversation with Eli, then with Hannah, and now with my mom. I've been stubbornly ignoring You. Not anymore.

Thank You for sending Hannah into my life. I will love her with my whole heart. Any fears I have, I will give them to You. Starting now. Watch over Eli. Guide the doctors to make the right decisions. His life is in Your hands.

The weight pressing down on his shoulders instantly became lighter. Ryker took a deep breath, the first one possible since Eli had been shot. Hannah had been right. Prayer was the place to start.

The doors leading to the emergency room swished open. Claire emerged. She came to a stop just inside the waiting room, her gaze sweeping across the various people. Tension practically poured from her.

Ryker handed Charlotte over to his mom and quickly crossed the room to her. "What is it?"

"Have you seen Hannah?"

Worry punctuated her words. Although she'd asked softly, their body language must've conveyed trouble because, within moments, they were surrounded by several members of Company A. Weston Donovan, Luke Tatum, and Bennett Knox joined them.

Ryker's gaze was locked on Claire. "Isn't she in the interview with Simon?"

"No. Simon gave me a list of places where Dusty might be hiding. I've been coordinating with my deputies to check them out. When I went back into the room, Bruce, Jose, and Gavin were there, but not Hannah. Bruce said he stepped into the hall with her, then went back into the room. That was about fifteen minutes ago." Her gaze swept across the men. "Have any of you seen her?"

Ryker knew with certainty she hadn't come into the waiting room. His hand balled into fists at the thought of Dusty getting anywhere near Hannah. "Something's happened to her."

Weston scraped a hand over his face. "Okay, let's not panic. She could be in the ladies' room or in the cafeteria grabbing something to eat. Ryker, go with Claire and check the surveillance cameras. The rest of us will split up and search the hospital room by room if we have to."

Five minutes later, nerves stretched tight, Ryker scanned the footage in the hospital's electronics room. Thirteen cameras were strategically placed around the emergency room and the nearby parking lots. The footage they captured was grainy. His gaze flickered from one to the other, searching for Hannah's copper-colored locks. Finally, he spotted her coming out of Simon's room with Bruce.

"There." He pointed to the screen. "Slow down. Follow that couple."

The technician did as he was told. Hannah and Bruce rounded a corner and disappeared from view.

"Do you have another shot of that hallway?" Claire asked.

"Afraid not. There's nothing down there except a supply closet and some bathrooms."

Frustration caused a swear word to rise on Ryker's tongue, but he held it back. Instead, he put his focus on the camera they did have. A few minutes later, Bruce reappeared and walked back to Simon's room. There was no sign of Hannah.

"Maybe she went into the bathroom," Claire suggested. "Let's keep watching until she reappears."

Ryker nodded, his attention glued to the screen. An orderly wearing scrubs and a mask wandered past, pushing an empty stretcher. He went down the hallway and disappeared from view. After two minutes, according to the timer on the footage, he returned, but this time a woman lay on the stretcher. Most of her face was covered by a sheet so it was impossible to know for sure, but Ryker had little doubt it was Hannah.

Beside him, Claire stiffened. She pointed to the man. "Correct me if I'm wrong, but that looks like Dusty."

Ryker peered at the screen. The criminal had chopped off his previously long hair, and the mask hid the bottom half of his face, but the identifiable scar creasing his neck peeked out from the collar of his scrubs. "He's changed his looks, but it's Dusty all right."

Dusty wheeled Hannah straight out of the emergency room to a loading dock for ambulances. Someone wearing a paramedic's uniform and a ball cap hopped out of the front seat and helped him load the gurney. As if the person knew the cameras were there, Dusty's accomplice purposefully kept his face hidden.

The two criminals hopped into the ambulance and tore off.

"Freeze that frame." Ryker pointed to the vehicle's license plate. Fulton County outfitted every one of their state vehicles with a tracking system. "We need a GPS location on that ambulance." He backed away from the door, yanking his keys from his pocket. "Text it to me, Claire."

"On it."

Ryker bolted from the room. The fastest way out of town from the hospital was northbound on the freeway. He instinctively knew that's the route Hannah's kidnappers had taken. Heading that way while Claire tracked the ambulance would give Ryker a head start. One he would need. Dusty was on a mission to kill Hannah.

Every second counted.

TWENTY-SIX

Shouting.

Hannah peeled her eyes open. Her gaze wouldn't focus. Darkness pressed in, the only illumination coming from a faint glow somewhere overhead. Her mouth was dry as a desert and her throat ached. The mattress underneath her was wrong. And those voices...they weren't familiar. Hannah couldn't make out the words, just the tenor of the conversation. It was tense.

She blinked, some primal instinct inside her blaring a desperate warning, and willed her gaze to focus. A haze clouded her thinking. Nothing about her surroundings made sense, and her hands hurt. She twisted her fingers. Fear jolted her heart into high gear. Her hands were bound with silver tape.

All at once, the last moments before she lost consciousness hit her. Hannah gasped and sat up. A wave of dizziness tilted her world one way and then the next. Her stomach threatened to revolt.

She slammed her eyes shut. Whatever drug Dusty had injected her with was still circulating in her system. Hannah took a deep breath. Then another. It slowed the course of adrenaline surging through her veins and stabilized her stomach. Gradually, her eyes adjusted to the dim lighting.

An ambulance. She was inside an ambulance.

Those angry voices were still outside. Her captors. Their voices were getting louder, as if they were approaching the rear doors. Her pulse skyrocketed. Frantically, Hannah searched her surroundings for some kind of weapon. Her gaze fell on a small pair of scissors, the kind typically used to cut through gauze. She grabbed them. Then tossed herself back onto the mattress seconds before the rear doors swung open.

Hannah winced as a flashlight beam shone in her face. Her heart beat hard enough to rattle her rib cage and her breathing grew shallow as a hulking figure climbed into the ambulance. Dusty. He sported several days' worth of growth on his chin and had chopped off his hair, but there was no mistaking the sneer on his face or the scar along his neck. In one hand, he carried a flashlight.

"She's awake." He addressed whoever he'd been arguing with earlier. "Of course she is. As if I don't have enough problems."

Dusty grabbed Hannah by the arm with a bruising grip before hauling her to her feet. She clutched the scissors in her bound hands, hiding them from view, as he shoved her toward the rear doors. Her gaze swept across their surroundings. Moonlight illuminated trees and a small road. They were in the middle of nowhere.

There were no streetlights. The ambulance was tilted, half of the wheels on the pavement and the other half in the dirt. Dusty shoved her. Thanks to the drugs in her system, Hannah's feet couldn't coordinate properly. She stumbled while trying to navigate the step on the back of the vehicle. Pain erupted along her shins as she tumbled to the hard-packed earth. Air whooshed from her lungs.

She lay stunned. A pair of tennis shoes appeared in her line of sight. Slowly, Hannah raised her gaze.

Shock vibrated through her.

Lorrie Michaels. Thomas's mistress was dressed in a paramedics uniform, her long hair tucked into a ball cap. She held a cell phone in one hand. She pointed it toward Hannah. "There she is, honey." Lorrie's voice was sticky sweet. "I promised you we'd be successful."

"I never doubted it." Thomas's voice spilled from the phone speaker.

Hannah's foggy mind tried to make sense of what was happening. Dusty and Lorrie were working together? They were doing Thomas's dirty work.

"The job is only half done," Dusty growled. "And if we don't get a move on, the cops are gonna find us before we can finish." He kicked a rear tire on the ambulance. It was flat. "The plan has fallen apart. This stupid thing has a tracker on it. We won't make it to the cabin before the cops arrive. Let's just kill her here and get it over with."

"No." Thomas's retort was sharp. "I want her killed

197

in the cabin like we discussed. The crimes have to look consistent. As if you're a serial killer, Dusty. My lawyer is close to getting Bruce to drop the charges. We need one final push."

They were discussing her murder in the same way some people argue over a restaurant. Fear threatened to choke Hannah. She battled it back, gripping the scissors in her hands. A clear head was her only way out of this. Dusty was right. The ambulance had a tracker on it. Someone would discover she was missing from the hospital, and hopefully, Ryker would discover how she'd been kidnapped.

Ryker. Her throat tightened at the thought of him. The memory of their kisses flashed in her mind. Hannah hadn't thought it was possible, but sometime over the last few days, she'd fallen in love with him. No... if she was honest, she'd started having feelings for him a long time ago.

She fought against it. Came up with every reason why a relationship wouldn't work out. But ultimately, none of that had mattered. Her heart refused to listen to reason. These last few days had merely forced her to recognize what was happening between them.

Tears pricked her eyes. If Dusty and Lorrie killed her, Ryker would blame himself. Just like he did when Alison died. Hannah couldn't bear the thought of that. She would fight. For herself. And for him.

But there was no guarantee her efforts would work.

Lord, my life is in Your hands. I ask for Your guidance

and Your wisdom. Give me the strength and the ability to survive this.

"I ain't going to prison for you, Thomas." Dusty's tone was hard as his lips curled into a sneer. He marched toward Lorrie until he was standing over her shoulder. "Do you hear me?"

"You won't get far without money," Thomas snapped. Then an audible sigh spilled from the cell phone speaker. "Do as we agreed and everything will fall into place. You'll be sipping cocktails on a Columbian beach surrounded by beautiful women by this time tomorrow."

"Fine." He handed his flashlight to Lorrie and then stormed over to Hannah. Once again, Dusty hauled her to her feet. The barrel of a gun jabbed into her side. "Don't give me a lick of trouble or I'll shoot you right here."

His breath was hot on her cheek and his tone was stone cold. He meant every word. Tension poured off his body like a tiger ready to pounce. Hannah didn't understand the relationship between Dusty and Lorrie, but she had the sense that he would shoot them both if need be. The only reason he hadn't was because of the money Thomas promised him. But if it came down to it... he would do what was necessary to save his own skin.

"Let's move, Lorrie." Dusty growled. "We're wasting time. The cabin is three miles away, and if I know Simon, he's already squealing like a piglet. It won't take long for the cops to figure out where we are once they find the ambulance."

"Honey, I'll call you when we get to the cabin so you

can watch Dusty kill her." Lorrie blew Thomas a kiss. "Love you."

Surreal. And twisted. Hannah didn't know which one of her captors was worse. Dusty, who had no problems killing an innocent person in cold blood, or Lorrie, who clearly was so enamored by Thomas she'd do anything for him.

Hannah gripped the scissors in her hand as Dusty steered her into the woods. He favored his left leg, probably due to the injury she'd given him with the screwdriver during the courthouse attack. Would that slow him down? She hoped so.

Hannah had three miles to figure out how to cut her binds without her captors realizing it. Then she had to escape. Once they reached the cabin, there wouldn't be another chance.

How much time had passed since they'd kidnapped her from the hospital? Did Ryker realize she was gone? Even if Hannah escaped from Dusty and Lorrie, where would she go? The questions swirled in her mind, threatening to drown her in worry and fear. Once again, she reminded herself that her life was in God's hand. She needed to focus on one thing at a time.

Leaves crunched under her feet as they entered the shelter of the trees. The moonlight faded, blocked by the canopy overhead. Hannah maneuvered the scissors in her hand until the blades were pressed against the tape binding her wrists together.

She started cutting.

TWENTY-SEVEN

Ryker slammed on his brakes as an ambulance came into view. The vehicle was parked on the side of the road with the bay doors hung open. There was no sign of Hannah. Or her captors.

Could she be in the front seat? Dead? The thought sent icicles of fear into his heart. He jerked the SUV into Park and ejected from the driver's seat.

Weston, who'd ridden with him from the hospital, was already five steps ahead. His colleague knew firsthand what it was like to have a loved one in danger. Weston's wife, Avery, had been hunted by a serial killer before they were married. Thankfully, she survived, and the couple were expecting their first baby any day, but the experience had been harrowing.

Weapon in hand, Weston circled the vehicle. Ryker took the other side. Moonlight, coupled with his vehicle's headlights, provided illumination. His heart double-timed as the front of the ambulance came into view. Weston shined a flashlight into the cab.

Empty.

Relief weakened Ryker's knees. It was short-lived. If Hannah wasn't here, then where was she? His gaze scanned the immediate area. There wasn't much to see. Thick forest lined the country road. "Did they switch vehicles?"

Weston circled the ambulance. "Maybe, but this tire is flat." He strolled the length of the road, his flashlight sweeping the area, and then came back. "No sign of tire tracks from another vehicle. I'm guessing something went awry with the plan when they got a flat tire."

Ryker flipped on his own flashlight and focused the beam on the grass. Some of the blades were indented as though they'd been trampled recently. It could've been an animal, but his instincts said it was Hannah and her captors. "I think they went the rest of the way on foot."

"Where?" Weston turned in a circle. Then he pulled out his cell phone and brought up the map. "There's nothing for miles."

"This is a hunting area. Could be a cabin." Ryker dialed Claire's number. She answered on the first ring. He quickly explained what they'd found. "You said Simon gave you a list of Dusty's hiding places. Is there anything within walking distance of our location?"

"Let me check."

Again, he was left standing around and waiting. Following Hannah and her captors through the woods wasn't possible without some indication of their direction. He didn't have enough tracking experience to see their trail. Especially not at night.

Ryker tried to hold it together, but the pressure building inside him was becoming harder to contain. A part of him wanted to cry. The other part wanted to punch something or someone until his knuckles bled. What was Dusty doing to Hannah? Was she in pain? Was she already dead?

She'd been with her captors for fifty-four minutes. A lot could happen in that time. Ryker had been a Texas Ranger long enough to know the horrible things people did to one another. He'd stood in Kristin's house, seen the blood staining her carpet and her bedsheets. Dusty was a cold-blooded killer.

He leaned against the hood of his SUV, head down. Tears pricked his eyes. He knew they were doing everything humanly possible to save Hannah, but what if it wasn't enough? It hadn't been for Alison. She'd died.

Prayer might help.

Hannah's words of wisdom replayed in Ryker's head. A reminder that just an hour ago, he'd promised to hand his fears to God. To surrender and accept that he could do his very best, but ultimately, Hannah's life was in God's hands.

A lump formed in his throat, and although Ryker knew he should pray, the words wouldn't come. He needed help. "Weston, can you pray for me?"

Weston placed a hand on his shoulder and squeezed. "Lord, we come to You with our pain. We know Hannah is not alone because You are with her, just as You are with us. Comfort us in our time of need. Help us be strong and guide our actions. Use us as instruments of Your goodness. In Your name, we pray."

"Amen." Ryker sucked in a deep breath and let it out slowly. His heart rate slowed, and although his muscles were still tense, Weston's words had shaved the edge off his anxiety. He kept the phone pressed to his ear, waiting for Claire to come back on with news.

Weston squeezed his shoulder again. "There's hope, man. The fact that they took her with them means they're working on some kind of plan."

Ryker nodded. His colleague was right. Dusty wanted Hannah dead, but hadn't killed her in the ambulance. There had to be a reason for that.

The sound of another vehicle approaching tightened his muscles, and his head swung up. He instantly relaxed when the driver came into view. Luke Tatum. His colleague exited the truck, along with Bennett Knox, another member of their team. The two men joined them. Weston quickly filled them in and a search of the ambulance and surrounding area began.

Bennett crouched to study the bent grass blades. Then he swung his flashlight beam into the woods. "I can track them."

Ryker's heart leapt into his throat. "You're sure?"

"Yep. My grandfather was one of the best trackers in the state. Taught me everything he knew. Based on the time it took us to drive from the hospital to this spot, they left the ambulance about thirty minutes ago. A healthy adult can walk three miles per hour, so that's a perimeter of a mile and a half."

"I've got supplies in my truck." Luke raced to his vehicle and pulled out an emergency backpack, along with several bottles of water.

"Ryker." Claire's voice came over his phone speaker. Her tone was clipped and urgent. "There's a cabin about three miles from your location on Simon's list. It's the only thing nearby within walking distance. I'm sending you the coordinates right now."

His phone beeped with a text message. Ryker's pulse jumped. If Bennett was correct, Dusty wouldn't have reached the cabin with Hannah yet. They were still traversing the woods. It was a simple decision. "I'm going with you, Bennett."

"Luke and I will go to the cabin," Weston said.

Ryker quickly texted the cabin's location to his colleague. "Between the two groups, we should find them. Stay in contact." He paused long enough to take in the members of his team. His brothers. Men who'd walk into danger with him without batting an eye, just like Eli had. "Be safe."

Luke and Weston both gave a sharp nod and then raced to the truck.

Ryker pulled his weapon and turned to Bennett. A sense of dread washed over him. The last man he'd gone into the woods with while chasing a suspect had been Eli. A mere five hours ago. His friend was still in surgery, fighting for his life.

This was dangerous, but there was no other option. Hannah needed them. "Lead the way, Bennett."

His colleague hitched up the backpack before sweeping his flashlight over the trees. He paused and then broke into a run. Ryker followed. The moonlight disappeared as they entered the forest.

Hold on, Hannah. We're coming.

TWENTY-EIGHT

Hannah stumbled. The blade sliced into her skin, and she smothered a yelp. Her fingers, slick with sweat and cramping from holding the scissors at a strange angle to cut her binds, nearly dropped the precious item. Dusty's grip on her arm was the only thing keeping her from falling. His hold tightened until she feared he'd cut off circulation to the rest of her arm.

"You're hurting me." She yanked in an attempt to pull away from him. The scissors had done a great job of cutting the tape around her wrists. Hannah was almost free. But she wouldn't get very far with Dusty's gun shoved in her kidney. Any escape attempt would be cut short by a bullet.

"Stop complaining." Dusty swore, following it up with a tirade about troublesome women.

"Shut up." Lorrie had lost the sweet tone to her voice now that she wasn't talking to Thomas. She'd been leading the way to the cabin, but stopped suddenly and turned. "I've had enough of your mouth. We wouldn't be in the situation if you'd handled business right the first time."

The expression that came over Dusty's face was frightening. Stone-cold. Flat. If he hadn't been holding on to her arm, Hannah would have shrunk away from him. For a moment, the gun held to her back wavered as if Dusty was considering shooting Lorrie.

The other woman either didn't pick up on his body language or she didn't care. Lorrie waved away a mosquito. "Pick up the pace. I want to get this over with."

Dusty muttered another curse word under his breath, but otherwise kept quiet. From the looks of things, Lorrie was calling the shots, but Hannah sensed that was only because of her connection to Thomas. Once Dusty got the money he was promised, all bets were off. Lorrie had a killer by the leash. One that would turn on her in an instant. And she didn't even have the brains to realize it.

Maybe Hannah could use that to her advantage. She needed a distraction. Creating an opportunity to escape was better than waiting for one. They must be getting close to the cabin. They'd been walking for about twenty minutes.

Was Ryker looking for her? She knew instinctively that he was. If Hannah got out of this alive, she would kiss him senseless. And then kiss him some more. She'd spent far too much time worried about where their relationship was leading to enjoy falling in love. Not anymore. Life was too short to let worry steal her joy.

She was in love with him. Hannah prayed she'd have the chance to tell him.

First, she had to get out of this. Hannah needed to focus on creating a distraction so she could escape. Every minute counted. It gave the Texas Rangers an opportunity to find her.

"You played me, Lorrie." Hannah carefully maneuvered over a root to keep from falling again. She used the movement to slice discreetly through more of the tape around her wrists with the scissor blade. "I truly thought you'd come to your senses about Thomas. Did you ever break up or was that just a ploy so you could act as the go-between for Thomas and Dusty?"

Lorrie chuckled. "Thomas and I love each other. Nothing can separate us. Not that stupid wife of his or the media or this ridiculous investigation." She cast a glowering look over her shoulder at Hannah. "You should have dropped the charges when you had the chance. Then none of this would've happened."

"He killed his wife."

"She was going to turn him into the police, the stupid woman. Thomas offered to pay for her silence, but she refused. Julie always did think she was better than everyone else."

Hannah didn't think turning her spouse in for breaking the law was a character flaw. She did find it laughable that Lorrie actually believed Thomas offered to buy Julie's silence. He would never take that risk. In fact, Hannah believed the good doctor had a plan for both

Dusty and Lorrie. One that would leave them both at the bottom of a grave.

Loose ends. That's what they were. And if Thomas had learned anything from killing his wife, it was to tie up loose ends.

Hannah cut a bit more. She was almost free. "Did you know Thomas and Dusty were running a drug scheme?"

"Of course. Who do you think helped Thomas enter the prescriptions into the system? We had a good thing going for a long time. Made a lot of money." She smirked at Dusty. "Some of us wasted it foolishly on gambling."

That explained why Dusty was willing to do Thomas's dirty work. Money and a guarantee of freedom. After all, Thomas could've flipped on Dusty and told the police everything about their drug business. Framed Dusty for Julie's murder.

Hannah's brow crinkled as something snapped into place. She inhaled sharply. "Thomas almost turned on you. The sketch created after Julie's death was released to the public. It was used to remind you of the power he had over you."

Dusty didn't answer, but his jaw tightened. It was enough to confirm Hannah was right.

Lorrie laughed. "Don't feel sorry for Dusty. He's making a ton of money out of this and is going to start a new life in a country under a different name. It's a win for everyone."

Hannah filled in the blanks on her own. Thomas offered Dusty money after threatening him. Then they created a plan to make it look like Dusty was responsible for Julie's murder. He broke into Hannah's house and attacked her. Called in the bomb threat at the courthouse. Murdered Kristin. Whatever it took to muddy the case. Hannah's stomach churned and bile rose in the back of her throat.

They all deserved to spend the rest of their lives in jail. Killers. Every one of them.

Lorrie was practically glowing. "My man is always three steps ahead of everyone else."

Dusty glowered. "If Thomas was so smart, he would've created a better alibi for himself and wouldn't have ended up the prime suspect."

The mirth faded from Lorrie's expression. "Watch your tone when you talk to me."

Dusty released Hannah and stepped in front of her to get into Lorrie's face. "I don't care if you are Thomas's girlfriend. No one disrespects me. No one. You'd better shut that mouth before I do it for you."

The couple began arguing. It was the opening Hannah had prayed for. She shrank back and sliced through the very last of her bonds. The movement must've caught Lorrie's eye because she stopped midsentence and pointed.

Hannah turned on her heel and bolted for cover.

A blaze of fire erupted along her side. She cried out and pressed a hand to her shirt. Warmth spouted from a wound near her stomach. Shot. She'd been shot. Her breath heaved as she kept moving despite the agony spreading through her body. Branches grabbed at her clothes and tree roots threatened to send her crashing to the ground. Sweat formed along her hairline. Her heartbeat roared in her ears.

Dusty was chasing her. Hannah could hear him coming. Panic swelled. If he caught her, he'd kill her. She knew that for certain.

Bark exploded from a pine tree next to her head. Hannah yelped and automatically ducked. She zigged and zagged to make herself a harder target to hit. Her vision blurred. She pressed a hand against the wound on her side, but couldn't apply any actual pressure. Blood seeped through her fingers and soaked her clothes. Her breath came in pants.

Move. Move. Move.

She put one foot in front of the other with no sense of direction. At one point, she'd been heading toward the road. Now she was all turned around. The pain in her body was blinding. She tripped, her knees crashing to the ground with a bone-jarring jolt that rattled through her body. Hannah pressed a hand against a nearby tree. She tried to get up. Willed her body to move. But it refused to obey. She sagged to the ground.

A bush shifted. Hannah whimpered and attempted to tuck herself into some foliage. Shivers racked her body.

Dusty appeared, chest heaving, his flashlight crossing over her hiding place. A sinister smile twisted his mouth as he raised the gun to shoot her. Hannah shut her eyes and said a final prayer of thanksgiving for every joyful moment God had given her.

Gunfire erupted.

TWENTY-NINE

"Why do they make this food so disgusting?" Hannah wrinkled her nose and pushed the mush on her hospital tray around with a bamboo fork. She glanced over at Eli's tray. Instead of sad-looking mush, he had fruit and chicken. Mashed potatoes with gravy. He even had a pudding cup. She scowled. "You don't have to eat the nasty stuff. That's not fair."

Eli arched his brows. "Actually, I did. It's part of the fun of abdominal surgery. The doctors sew your insides back together and then you have to eat soft food until you graduate to decent stuff." He picked up his pudding. "Don't be such a whiner. Eat your food like a good patient so we can go on a walk together."

Hannah narrowed her gaze at him. "Stop bossing me around." She was dying for some actual food, abdominal surgery or not. It'd been three days since her harrowing experience in the woods. She was grateful to be alive, but not happy about her culinary options, especially when

Eli took a huge bite of his pudding. "I don't like eating lunch with you."

"Eli, are you annoying Hannah again?" Ryker's father appeared in the doorway with a bouquet tucked in a vase. Jack squinted at the younger man. "Don't make me beat you over the head with your walker."

Unfazed by the empty threat, Eli shoveled another spoonful of pudding into his mouth. "I'm not mean. I'm just telling her how it is."

Hannah's breath stalled as Ryker entered behind his father. He wore a soft T-shirt that molded over his broad chest and brought out the green highlights in his hazel eyes. Since he was off duty, he wasn't sporting his ranger badge or gun, but it didn't matter. Ryker carried himself like a lawman. It was in his stride and assessing gaze.

They'd only been separated for an hour. Just long enough for Ryker to run home for a shower and a decent meal. He'd been planted next to her bedside since the rescue operation. He'd saved her from Dusty. Ryker had shot the criminal twice before he could fire at Hannah. Dusty was seriously injured, but survived.

Hannah was in terrible shape by the time the medics arrived to help her. Dusty's bullet had ripped through her abdomen. It'd taken two surgeries to put her back together, but the doctors believed she'd make a full recovery.

Ryker's expression warmed as he approached her bedside. "Hey there, beautiful."

Hannah's cheeks heated. Ryker's lips turned up into an easy smile before he tilted down to sweep a kiss across her mouth. The heart monitor she was hooked up to blipped. Her blush deepened as she realized everyone in the room knew just how much her pulse increased the moment Ryker was near.

She was tempted to hide under the covers from embarrassment, but then he ran a hand over her hair and kissed her again. Just a simple brush of his lips, but the monitor's beeping increased again.

"If you two keep that up," Eli said. "A nurse is gonna come running in here thinking Hannah's having some kind of attack."

Ryker shot his best bud a glare, but there was no heat behind it and a smile played on his lips. "You're gonna be the one who needs a nurse if you don't cut out the commentary."

Eli snorted. "I can still take you down even after surgery."

"No one is taking anyone down." Zoe strolled into the room with Charlotte on her hip. She caught Hannah's gaze and then rolled her eyes. "I thought this kind of behavior would stop when they became adults, but nope. They're like toddlers some days."

Hannah chuckled and then held her side as the stitches pulled. "Don't make any jokes. It still hurts to laugh."

She lifted hands to show she wanted Charlotte. The little girl wore a unicorn T-shirt and matching pants. Her dark hair was tucked into a bow at the top of her head. When Zoe obliged and settled the baby on the bed,

Hannah cuddled her close. She smothered Charlotte's face with kisses. "I missed you so much."

Charlotte giggled. The sound reached in and wrapped itself around Hannah's heart. She kissed the baby again, causing another peel of laughter. Her niece looked happy and healthy. Well loved. Hannah lifted her gaze to meet Zoe's. "Thank you so much for taking such good care of her."

"The pleasure is all mine." Zoe patted her hand and then smiled brightly at Charlotte. "This little girl is a bright ray of sunshine. I've enjoyed having her with me."

"The doctor says if everything goes well, I should be released in a couple of days." Despite Zoe's kind words, Hannah couldn't help but feel guilty for the burden she'd placed on the Montgomery family. She didn't want to take advantage of their generosity. "Charlotte and I—"

"Will stay on the ranch until you fully recover." Zoe arched a brow, as if daring Hannah to argue. "You're going to let me cook for you and help with Charlotte and do anything else you need." She hooked an arm around her husband's waist. "Jack and I have already discussed it. We're in agreement."

"Now, my love, you're being pushy again." Jack smiled down at Zoe lovingly. "Hannah should make her own decision about the matter."

"It's easier if you just give in," Eli injected. "Otherwise, Zoe will show up at your door every day with food and stay for hours taking care of Charlotte." He grinned. "We'll be patients together. Zoe already offered me a spare bedroom on the ground floor. We'll amuse each other with movies and board games."

Hannah groaned. "That sounds like a reason to avoid staying on the ranch."

Everyone laughed. She winked at Eli to take the sting out of her words, and he stuck a tongue out in response. The move made her laugh, and she winced as pain sliced her wounds. Hannah leaned her head against the pillow. Exhaustion swept over her like a tidal wave. Her energy levels were still low after surgery.

Zoe noticed and swept Charlotte into her arms. "I think it's time to let you rest, Hannah. We'll come back and see you later."

"Come on." Jack retrieved Eli's walker and helped him into a standing position. "I'll race you down the hallway."

"You're on, old man." Eli grinned.

Their good-natured teasing continued as they left the room.

Hannah took Ryker's hand. "Your family is wonderful."

He perched on the edge of her bed. "They are." He rubbed a thumb over her knuckles. "Mom is serious about her offer. The decision is yours, of course, but I don't think you'll be allowed to lift Charlotte even after you're released from the hospital given your injuries. It makes sense for you to stay on the ranch until you recover fully."

"You have a point. I just hate to be a burden."

Ryker met her gaze. "You're never a burden. Besides,

what else is family for? We're supposed to take care of each other."

"Except I'm not a Montgomery."

He opened his mouth to reply, but a knock at the door cut him off. Ryker rose from the bed just as Claire and Gavin entered. The couple were dressed in their respective uniforms. Claire's hair was slicked back and tucked under a cowboy hat, her duty belt loaded down with her holster, cuffs, and pepper spray. The sheriff's badge pinned to her chest shone in the fluorescent lighting. Gavin looked every inch of the Texas Ranger in his button-down shirt, cowboy boots, and tan hat. Matching his-and-her wedding bands encircled their left fingers.

Hannah's chest tightened. Claire and Gavin had been working on the investigation over the last few days since the incident in the woods. From the grim looks on their faces, this wasn't a social visit.

"Hey, guys." Ryker shook Gavin's hand before doing the same with Claire. Then he crossed back to Hannah's bedside and placed a comforting hand on her shoulder.

Gavin's gaze softened. "How are you feeling, Hannah?"

"Better, thanks. The doctors say I should be able to bust out of here in a few days."

"Glad to hear it."

"We're sorry to disturb you." Claire removed her cowboy hat and held it in one hand. "But we've made headway on the investigation and wanted you to hear things from us before some industrious reporter blasts it all over the news." Her grim expression relaxed into a smile. "We got them. All of them. You're safe, Hannah. It's over."

She blinked, hardly able to believe it. "What? Seriously?"

Gavin nodded. "Thomas, Dusty, and Lorrie were the only ones involved in the drug scheme and the murders of Julie and Kristin. Dusty confessed to everything in a plea bargain deal yesterday. He'll spend the rest of his life in prison, but one with minimum security so his mom can visit him."

"Dusty and Thomas created the drug scheme?" Ryker asked.

"Yes. Dusty provided names and then Thomas would write electronic prescriptions using his wife's information. The individuals would fill those prescriptions at the pharmacy, get their narcotics, and then turn them over to Dusty for a small fee. He'd sell them on the street. It was a profitable business, one they had for a long time."

"Until Julie found out."

Claire nodded. "According to Dusty, Thomas suspected Julie had uncovered his prescription drug scheme. That was confirmed when she confronted him. Thomas devised a plan to kill her and cover his tracks with the grocery store run." She put grocery store in quotes to show it was a fake alibi. "He would've gotten away with it, too, except Ryker didn't stop digging. The affair he'd been having with Lorrie was discovered and we figured that was his motive for killing her."

"My screw-up." Ryker grimaced. "I should've dug harder into Julie. Maybe then I would've uncovered the unusual number of pain prescriptions attached to her name."

"You didn't know to look for it," Gavin countered. "No one—not even her family or colleagues—knew what she suspected was happening at the office. She kept quiet because Julie thought her husband was behind it and wasn't certain what she'd do about it."

"It's not easy to turn in someone you love." Hannah had sympathy for family members of criminals. Doing the right thing often meant turning on someone you cared deeply about. "I'm sorry Julie never got the chance to go to the police. In the end, she wanted to do the right thing and was killed for it."

Claire nodded. "After Thomas was charged, he devised a plan for Dusty to get him out of the murder charge. Initially, Dusty refused."

Hannah already knew this part. "That's when Thomas went to Ryker with that made-up story about being attacked in the parking lot of his office. The sketch of his attacker was designed to frighten Dusty into submission. Thomas purposefully left off the scar, but wanted Dusty to know he could add it later."

"Exactly. Dusty was forced to help him."

Again she used air quotes around forced. Dusty had options. He could've gone to the police and confessed to what he'd done. Instead, he attacked Hannah and killed Kristin.

"Dusty is the one who broke into your house, Hannah." Gavin rocked back on his heels. "He's behind the courthouse attack, running ya'll off the road, and killing Kristin. Every order Thomas gave was passed through Lorrie. She acted as the go-between, so we couldn't find any communication between Thomas and Dusty."

Hannah blew out a breath. "She had me completely fooled. I really thought she'd figured out her mistakes."

"She had us all fooled." Ryker gently squeezed her shoulder. "It's strange. Why didn't Dusty just kill Thomas? It would've been easier than plotting to kill Hannah."

"Because of Lorrie. She knew everything, so Dusty would've had to kill her too. Additionally, Thomas had given his lawyer a sealed envelope containing documents that explained everything. His instructions to Jose were to open it only if he was ever killed. Dusty couldn't take the risk."

"What about Bruce? And Jose? Were they involved in any of this?"

"No. Jose truly believed Thomas was innocent. Since he and Bruce are friends, Jose pushed to have the case dropped. Bruce told us he was succumbing to the stress of everything. He worried about how he was being portrayed in the media. Pam's discussion with him served as a reminder that, as District Attorney, his priority needed to be the truth."

Hannah was relieved to hear her faith in her boss wasn't misguided. And she was grateful to her paralegal for sticking up for her. "I need to give Pam an enormous box of chocolates."

Claire laughed. "I think we all deserve chocolate

after this." Her expression grew serious again. "Jose was horrified to learn Thomas had played him."

Ryker rocked back on his heels. "So he was telling the truth about not recognizing Dusty?"

"Seems so. Jose was going through a divorce back then and explained he was an emotional wreck. That entire year of his life was a blur." Claire frowned. "When Lorrie and Thomas were confronted with the evidence against them, they both confessed as well. There won't be a trial. Neither of them will see the outside of a prison cell."

Another wave of relief crashed over Hannah. She was prepared to face her attackers from the witness stand, but it was nice to know that it wasn't necessary. "Thank you, Claire. And Gavin. Words can't express my appreciation."

"We only did our jobs." Claire patted her foot. "You deserve all the credit. It would've been easy to drop the charges against Thomas, but you stuck it out even through being threatened and injured. Few others would have done so."

"Not true. It was the right thing to do. That's all." Hannah reached up to grab Ryker's hand, which was still resting on her shoulder. "None of us gave up and justice was done. It won't bring Julie or Kristin back, but I hope it gives their families some measure of comfort."

Claire and Gavin chatted with them a bit longer, but when Hannah stifled a yawn, they left.

Once again, she leaned against the pillows. Exhaustion was really tugging at her. Still, she interlaced her fingers with Ryker's and patted the bed to indicate he should retake his position next to her. He obliged by doing something better. He angled half of his frame onto the mattress and pulled her into his arms.

Hannah sighed with contentment as she snuggled up in his warm embrace. "I'm so glad it's all over."

"Me too." He brushed a kiss across the top of her head before leaning his cheek against it. "That means there's just one more order of business to take care of. I know you're tired, so I'll keep it short, but I can't hold in what I have to say anymore." He pulled back and tilted her face up until she was staring into his eyes. "I love you, Hannah."

She inhaled sharply. With everything going on, they hadn't discussed their relationship. She'd known Ryker cared about her, but she hadn't realized his feelings ran as deep as hers. "You do?"

"Yes. And I know you aren't a Montgomery today, but I need you to know that I fully intended on making you one in the not-so-distant future." Worry tangled with the love in his expression. "That is, if you'll have me."

Tears flooded her vision. They spilled over her lashes onto her cheeks. For years, she'd prayed for a man like Ryker to come into her life. Hannah wouldn't let anything stop her from accepting God's blessings. "Of course I'll have you. I love you too, Ryker."

His breath hitched as his own eyes grew cloudy with emotion. Ryker gently, ever so gently, captured her lips with his. An explosion of feelings rocked Hannah to her core. She relished them. Her future was with this man, and she was grateful for the love they shared.

When the kiss ended, they were both breathless. Hannah brushed her lips against his once more. Her heart monitor beeped at a rapid pace. She smiled. "Eli's right. Some nurse is gonna come in here thinking I'm having a heart attack if you keep kissing me like that."

"Let 'em come in." Ryker ran a thumb over her cheek. "Cuz, sweetheart, I have no plan on stopping. I'm gonna be kissing you like that for the rest of our lives."

The rest of their lives. Hannah's heart swelled with the thought.

A whole life with Ryker by her side was perfect.

THIRTY

Eight months later

Ryker weaved his way through his parents' house. The balcony doors leading to the yard were wide open, letting in the crisp night air and the fragrant scent of roses from the nearby flower beds. Music blared from the indoor/outdoor speakers. A dance floor was set up in the grass. Guests—family and friends—were gathered together for the annual Montgomery New Year's Eve party.

He spotted Ben and Danielle standing together with their daughter, Charlotte. Hannah's brother and sister-in-law had made it home safely from their deployments and were happily reunited with their little girl. Since their return, Ryker had gotten to know the couple well. He found them kind, caring, and dedicated.

Charlotte was dressed in pajamas, but there was no

hint of sleepiness in her face. She reached for Ryker the moment he approached. He happily scooped her into his arms. "What are you still doing up?"

"She slept for a while and then woke up on her own." Danielle smiled lovingly at her daughter. "I didn't have the heart to put her back to bed. It seems fitting that we ring in the new year all together." She wrapped an arm around her husband's waist. "As a family."

Ryker could appreciate the sentiment. Ben and his wife had spent most of the year apart on separate deployments. Their commitment to the military was admirable, especially given the hardship it created for them personally. He deeply admired the couple.

"I agree." He kissed Charlotte's cheek before handing her back to her mom. "Speaking of ringing in the New Year, has anyone seen my lovely wife? She's disappeared."

Wife. Ryker loved the way that word rolled off his tongue. He and Hannah were married a week before Thanksgiving. Time had only deepened their devotion. Ryker wasn't sure how it was possible, but he fell more and more in love with Hannah every day. She brought a happiness to his life he'd never experienced before.

Ben's brow crinkled. "I saw her heading upstairs a little while ago."

"I'll go check on her. Thanks."

He headed for the staircase but came up short when he spotted Eli on the landing. The man was holding a card and staring off into space. His mouth was drawn tight. Time and physical therapy had helped Eli to heal from his gunshot wounds, but he was still on medical leave from the rangers. The doctors wanted him to wait a few more weeks before returning to full duty.

Ryker joined his friend. "Hey, you okay?"

Eli blinked. "I'm fine." He lifted the card in his hand. "It's from Sienna. Your mom got it yesterday in the mail. I guess Sienna didn't know where else to send it."

He took the card from his buddy and scanned the contents. It was a get-well card. Nothing about the note to Eli from his ex-fiancée was terribly personal, but the message was kind. Sienna wished him happiness and hope for the new year.

Ryker handed it back with a sigh. He didn't know exactly what happened between Eli and Sienna, only that they'd broken up. Five years had passed, but Eli still refused to talk about it. Whatever happened, it'd scarred him. Ryker didn't like seeing his friend so heartbroken. "Maybe it's time to reach out to her. See if you can mend some of the fences that were broken."

Eli's jaw tightened. "No. What's done is done." He shrugged. "The card just threw me for a loop, that's all."

Ryker debated digging deeper into the conversation, but he could tell from the stubborn tilt of Eli's chin that his friend didn't want to discuss it. Probably better to let it go for now. They were in the middle of a party. That made a heart-to-heart difficult.

He clapped a hand on Eli's shoulder. "If you ever need someone to listen, I'm here."

"I know. Thanks."

Eli bounded down the stairs and rejoined the party.

Ryker continued to the second floor. His old bedroom door was cocked open. He poked his head in. "Hannah?"

She was seated on the bed. His wife was gorgeous in a dress that skated along her beautiful curves and brought out the copper highlights in her hair. She rose quickly with a smile that made his heart skip a beat. For a moment, Ryker was struck with how out of place she looked there among his high school trophies and old posters.

Ryker kissed her softly. "You disappeared from the party."

"Sorry, I just needed a quiet moment." Her gaze skipped around the bedroom. A smile played on her lips. "You know, your mom once mentioned after we were married that she would turn this room into a nursery once we started having kids."

"That sounds like her. She's been biting her tongue, but I know she's eager for grandkids. She plans to spoil them rotten."

Hannah wrapped her arms around his waist. "Well, in about nine months, we're all going to have someone to smother in love and hugs."

Ryker's heart stopped and then took off like a shot as her words sank into him. Then he yelled with joy and picked Hannah up before spinning her around. He set her down on the carpet and pulled away to eye her up and down. Her figure looked exactly the same, but she radiated with a fresh glow of happiness. How had he missed that?

"You're really pregnant?" He had to hear the words again. "We're having a baby? You're sure?"

She laughed. "Yes, we're having a baby. Next year will be very exciting." She wrapped her arms around his neck. "Congratulations, Ryker. You're gonna be a daddy."

"I thought nothing would be better than being called your husband. But daddy... that's... wow." Ryker kissed her with all the passion and joy that couldn't be expressed in words. Hannah was going to be a fantastic mother. He couldn't wait to start this next adventure with her. He pulled away only long enough to whisper three little words. "I love you."

ALSO BY LYNN SHANNON

Texas Ranger Heroes Series

Ranger Protection

Ranger Redemption

Ranger Courage

Ranger Faith

Ranger Honor

Triumph Over Adversity Series

Calculated Risk

Critical Error

Necessary Peril

Strategic Plan

Covert Mission

Tactical Force

Would you like to know when my next book is released? Or when my novels go on sale? It's easy. Subscribe to my newsletter at www.lynnshannon.com and all of the info will come straight to your inbox!

Reviews help readers find books. Please consider leaving a review at your favorite place of purchase or anywhere you discover new books. Thank you.

Made in the USA
Middletown, DE
03 August 2024

58459914R00145